Twisted Pearl of The Prairies
By
RACHEL MANN

This is a work of fiction. Similarities to real people, places, or events are entirely coincidental.

TWISTED PEARL OF THE PRAIRIES

First edition. December 8, 2024.

Copyright © 2024 Rachel Mann.

ISBN: 979-8227086297

Written by Rachel Mann.

Table of Contents

Preface 1
Chapter 1: The Meeting 3
Chapter 2: The Allure 9
Chapter 3: The Discovery 21
Chapter 4: Control 35
Chapter 4 : Returning Home 45
Chapter 5: Alex left abruptly 49
Chapter 6: It was Christmas 82
Chapter 6: Elena's New Beginning 84
Chapter 7: A new horizon 89
Chapter 8: The Awakening 92
Epilogue 94

To my special grain of sand...

"The most profound journeys are not those measured in miles, but in the courage to walk away from what dims your light and toward the truth of who you are."—Anonymous

Preface

In the ever-shifting landscape of human relationships, exists a subtle yet profound interplay between love and control. When entangled with a narcissistic partner, one can lose sight of their own essence, becoming ensnared in the illusions of the ego. "Twisted Pearl of The Prairies" explores this dynamic through the lens of consciousness, inspired by the teachings of Eckhart Tolle in "The Power of Now" and "A New Earth".

Narcissism, rooted deeply in the unconscious ego, distorts the very nature of love. It creates a mirror that reflects not truth, but a carefully curated illusion. Those who fall under its spell often find their sense of self eroded by the constant need for approval and the insidious control of their partner.

Elena Foster's journey is an awakening, loss, and ultimate liberation. It is a story of how the egoic mind, when left unchecked, can wield love as a tool for manipulation and domination. But it is also a tale of hope, of discovering the power of presence and reclaiming one's true identity.

Through Elena's experiences, we witness the magnetic allure of a narcissistic partner, the charm that conceals a darker intent. We see the gradual erosion of her self-worth, the isolation, and the manipulation that keeps her bound to Adrian Blackwood. Yet, we also see her awakening to the present moment, her courage to confront the painful truth, and her determination to heal through consciousness.

"Twisted Pearl of The Prairies" is more than a narrative of a toxic relationship; it is a testament to the transformative power of awareness. It is a reminder that true love is rooted in presence, not in the ego's illusions and that no one should ever be made to feel less than their true self.

This book is dedicated to those who have found themselves overshadowed by a narcissist, to those who have felt the sting of emotional manipulation, and to those who have courageously broken free to discover their inner light. May Elena's story inspire you to transcend the reflections of the ego and awaken to the profound reality of your consciousness.

Chapter 1: The Meeting

Tinder and the plethora of dating apps this is how we meet our potential life partner nowadays. Gone were those days when courtship was so authentic with a girl or a guy from the local bar, the same village or the classroom next door.

It was no different for Elena, she was an expatriate in Hong Kong at that time and she went through an awfully difficult divorce but seeing it is a norm in the modern society with the leap of faith and hope to find love again she gave the app a shot. While she felt plentiful of embarrassment to even sign up, many of her friends were sharing that they were all doing that too.

Constant swiping, chats and dates; brought her nowhere but to learn more deceit and lies. I guess we have all seen the recent Tinder movies *"Tinder Swindler"*, *"Love, Stalker, Killer"*, "Love Me Tinder", while conscious and alert about the reality, the question is where else or how else do you meet people? It is all about hiding behind the screens! This is the new world we live in, a digital social society.

Elena hesitated as her finger hovered over the screen. The soft glow of her phone illuminated her features, a mix of doubt and curiosity flickering across her face. Another swipe, another match—what could possibly change this time?

The profile stared back at her: Alex, 38, prairie-born and world-traveled. His warm smile was disarming, but it was his bio that intrigued her. *"Dreamer by heart, realist by choice. Lover of books, wanderer of paths unknown."*

She swiped right, her heart thudding as the screen flashed, *"It's a match!"*

Alex's first message came within minutes, a thoughtful response to one of her favorite books listed on her profile. *"Haruki Murakami is a master of turning the mundane into magic. 'Norwegian Wood' made me rethink how love shapes us. What's your take?"*

Elena smiled despite herself. Their conversation flowed effortlessly, like two old friends reconnecting after years apart. He asked about her dreams, her struggles, her favorite songs. His words carried a warmth that felt almost tangible.

Yet, even in those early exchanges, there were subtle moments that lingered in the back of her mind. When she mentioned her busy schedule, Alex teased, *"I hope you'll carve out time for someone who really gets you. We all need someone like that, don't we?"* His tone was playful, but something about the comment stuck with her—an unspoken expectation, a thread of possessiveness masked as interest.

Three weeks passed in a whirlwind of messages, playlists, and shared photos of daily life. Alex had a knack for making her feel seen, his attention both comforting and intoxicating. But beneath the charm, Elena sometimes felt a quiet unease she couldn't quite name—a sense that Alex wasn't just trying to understand her but shape her world to include only him.

When the time came to meet, Elena felt a mix of anticipation and trepidation. As she entered the hotel lobby where Alex waited, she spotted him instantly. He stood near the entrance, his tall frame leaning casually against the wall, a bouquet of wildflowers in hand.

"Elena," he greeted, his smile warm and familiar, as if they'd known each other forever.

She smiled back, allowing herself to believe—if only for a moment—that this could be the start of something extraordinary.

For the next three weeks, Elena and Alex's Tinder conversations became the highlight of her days. Each morning began with a cheerful

"Good morning" message from Alex, his words infused with a warmth that made her smile before she even got out of bed. They quickly moved beyond the superficial small talk that so often characterized online dating. Instead, their messages were deep and meaningful, touching on everything from childhood memories to future aspirations.

Elena found herself eagerly anticipating their evening exchanges, where they would dive into long discussions about their favourite books, the places they dreamed of travelling, and their shared love for food and indie music. They sent each other song recommendations, creating a playlist that became the soundtrack of their growing bond. Every song had a story, a reason why it resonated with them, and sharing these personal tidbits brought them closer.

Alex had a way of making Elena feel seen and understood. He remembered the little details she mentioned in passing and would bring them up later, showing her that he genuinely listened and cared. When she had a rough day at work, his supportive messages made everything feel more manageable. They shared jokes, exchanged silly memes, and even sent each other photos of their day-to-day lives, bridging the gap between their digital conversations and the real world.

By the end of the three weeks, what started as a casual connection had blossomed into something much deeper. Elena felt a sense of intimacy and trust with Alex that she hadn't experienced in a long time. The distance between them, once a mere geographical fact, now felt like a minor obstacle they were eager to overcome. Their bond was undeniable, and both of them knew it was only a matter of time before their virtual connection would translate into a real-life meeting, where their burgeoning feelings could truly take flight.

The day arrived when Alex, filled with nervous excitement and anticipation, boarded a plane that would take him from his small town in the Prairies to the picturesque island where Elena lived. As he settled into his seat, his mind raced with thoughts of their three weeks of deep conversations and shared moments. The connection they had forged online felt so real, yet Alex couldn't shake a hint of apprehension about meeting Elena face-to-face. Alex almost couldn't make this trip as he was terribly ill while returning to his city after a business trip in Ukraine. He was thinking hard about whether he'd wants to take another flight as he was literally sitting right next to the toilet his entire flight returning.

Meanwhile, on the island, Elena paced nervously in her apartment overlooking the turquoise waters. She had butterflies in her stomach, a mix of excitement and a touch of doubt. What if their chemistry didn't translate offline? What if their expectations didn't align with reality? But amidst these thoughts, Elena couldn't deny the thrill of finally meeting the man who had captured her heart through their heartfelt exchanges.

Hours later, Alex's plane touched down on the island, and he made his way through the bustling airport with a racing heart. He checked into a hotel as Elena wasn't able to pick him up but they agreed to meet at the hotel.

He spotted Elena waiting for him at the lobby, her smile radiant and her eyes sparkling with anticipation. Their eyes met, and in that moment, any doubts melted away. They embraced tightly, the warmth of their hug confirming what their hearts already knew: this was the beginning of something special.

Together, they explored the island hand in hand, sharing laughter, stories, and stolen glances that spoke volumes. They visited quaint cafes overlooking the sea, walked along secluded beaches as the sun dipped below the horizon, and found quiet moments to simply be together. With each passing day, their connection deepened, and the digital bond they had nurtured bloomed into a beautiful reality.

As they watched the waves crash against the shore one evening, Alex turned to Elena and whispered, "I'm so glad I took that flight." Elena smiled softly, her heart overflowing with gratitude for the leap of faith they had both taken. In that tranquil moment, surrounded by the beauty of the island and the promise of their newfound love, they knew that their journey together was only just beginning.

A few days passed in a whirlwind of discovery and intimacy for Alex and Elena on the island. Every moment spent together seemed fleeting yet profound, each shared experience strengthening their bond. But as their time together neared its end, reality intruded in the form of Alex's impending departure back to his small town.

Standing on the same beach where they had shared their first sunset, Alex held Elena close, his heart heavy with the knowledge that he would soon have to leave. They talked late into the night, their conversations weaving between dreams for the future and the bittersweet reality of their impending separation.

Elena listened intently as Alex shared his plans and responsibilities waiting for him back home. He spoke passionately about his work, his family, and the community he cherished, giving Elena a deeper glimpse into the man she had grown to care for deeply. Despite the physical distance that would soon separate them, they vowed to keep their connection alive through daily messages, late-night calls, and plans for future visits.

Their dialogue became even more intense and intimate in the days leading up to Alex's departure. They poured their hearts out, sharing fears, hopes, and aspirations with a vulnerability that deepened their emotional connection. Each message exchanged carried the weight of longing and anticipation, a testament to the strength of their bond and their commitment to nurture it despite the miles between them.

As Alex boarded the plane back home, he carried with him memories of sun-drenched days and starlit nights spent with Elena. The feeling of her hand in his, the sound of her laughter, and the depth of their conversations remained etched in his mind, reassuring him that their love would endure the distance. And as he looked out of the plane window, he knew that this brief chapter on the island was just the beginning of a love story that was meant to unfold across time and space.

Chapter 2: The Allure

As the weeks passed, Elena found herself increasingly immersed in Alex's world. His charm and attentiveness were magnetic, drawing her deeper into their shared conversations about art, literature, and their aspirations. Alex had a remarkable ability to make Elena feel like the most important person in his life, his genuine interest in her thoughts and feelings creating a sense of intimacy she had longed for.

Elena and Alex's bond deepened with each passing day, their conversations often veering into the profound. He had a way of making her feel like the center of his universe, his eyes lighting up as she spoke about her dreams and childhood.

But every now and then, there were moments that sent an unexplainable chill through her. Like the time they were at a café, and a waiter accidentally spilled a glass of water near their table. Alex's jaw tightened, his smile vanishing as he snapped at the young man. "Do you even pay attention to what you're doing?" he said coldly.

Elena felt a twinge of discomfort. Alex apologized for his tone immediately after, brushing it off as frustration from a long day. Yet, the incident lingered in her mind.

Another time, during a dinner with her close friend Lily, Alex dominated the conversation. His charm was undeniable, but when Lily asked Elena a question, Alex cut her off mid-sentence, redirecting the focus back to himself.

Later that night, Elena brought it up hesitantly. "You were a little dismissive with Lily."

Alex sighed, pulling her close. "I didn't mean to be. Sometimes I just get excited. Besides, she was asking silly questions—you deserve better than that."

Elena nodded, but a quiet voice in the back of her mind asked: *Why did he need to take over? Why did he dismiss her friend so easily?*

These moments were fleeting but left behind a trace of unease. It was as though Alex's warmth could turn to ice in an instant, his charm masking something darker.

When Alex's business trip took him through several European cities, Elena seized the opportunity to join him on this adventure of exploration and love. Their journey began in Paris, where they wandered along the Seine, marvelling at the iconic architecture of the Louvre and strolling through Montmartre's charming streets. They shared croissants in quaint cafes, sipped coffee overlooking the bustling streets, and whispered secrets in the shadow of the Eiffel Tower at night.

From Paris, they traveled to Barcelona, where the vibrant energy of Gaudi's whimsical architecture captivated them. They spent lazy afternoons at the beach, soaking in the Mediterranean sun, and indulged in tapas and sangria at lively outdoor markets. In the evenings, they danced under the stars to flamenco rhythms, their laughter mingling with the passionate music that echoed through the narrow alleys of the Gothic Quarter.

Their next stop was Rome, where history unfolded at every turn. They stood awestruck in the grandeur of the Colosseum, tossed coins into the Trevi Fountain for good luck, and shared gelato on the steps of the Spanish Steps. In Vatican City, they marveled at the artistry of Michelangelo's Sistine Chapel ceiling and whispered in reverence in the hushed corridors of St. Peter's Basilica.

As they journeyed from city to city, Elena and Alex discovered new facets of each other's personalities and deepened their bond. In each location, they found moments of quiet intimacy and exhilarating adventure, forging memories that would last a lifetime. Whether savoring paella in Valencia, exploring the canals of Venice, or marveling at the beauty of Prague's old town, their hearts intertwined with the joy of discovery and the warmth of shared experiences.

By the time they boarded the plane back home, their suitcases filled with souvenirs and their hearts overflowing with memories, Elena and Alex knew that this journey had not only enriched their relationship but had also laid a foundation for a future filled with love, adventure, and endless possibilities.

During their travels across Europe, Alex's business trip coincided with a pivotal company function in London, providing the perfect opportunity for Elena to witness another side of his life. As they arrived at the elegant venue overlooking the Thames, Elena felt a mix of excitement and nerves, dressed in a sleek gown that Alex had complimented her on earlier.

Alex introduced Elena to his business acquaintances with a pride that warmed her heart. She observed how effortlessly he navigated conversations, his demeanor shifting from the carefree explorer she had seen in the cities to the composed professional guiding her through the room. Each introduction was accompanied by genuine enthusiasm as he shared stories of their travels and highlighted Elena's accomplishments and interests.

Elena, in turn, felt a sense of belonging as she engaged in conversations with Alex's colleagues, discussing their shared passions for art, literature, and travel. She marveled at Alex's ability to seamlessly blend his personal and professional worlds, seeing firsthand the respect and admiration he garnered from those around him.

Throughout the evening, Alex's attentiveness never wavered. He made sure Elena felt included, guiding her through the intricacies of business discussions and seamlessly integrating her into the social fabric of the event. Their shared glances across the room spoke volumes, a silent acknowledgment of the deeper connection they had forged beyond the glittering surface of the occasion.

As they bid farewell to Alex's colleagues at the end of the night, Elena felt a surge of pride and affection for the man who had brought her into his world with such grace and sincerity. Walking hand in hand through the illuminated streets of London, their hearts full of shared experiences and newfound admiration, Elena knew that this night had solidified their bond in ways that transcended the glamour of the event itself.

As their European adventure came to an end, Elena and Alex returned to their respective cities, but their connection continued to flourish digitally. They exchanged daily messages filled with longing and excitement, reminiscing about their favorite moments from the trip and planning future adventures together.

Despite the physical distance, their conversations deepened in intimacy and honesty. They shared their dreams, fears, and aspirations with a vulnerability that only strengthened their bond. Late-night video calls became their refuge, where they could laugh, discuss deep topics, and gaze into each other's eyes across the screen, feeling as close as if they were in the same room.

Their digital connection became a lifeline, bridging the miles between them with words of affection and gestures of support. They sent each other songs that reminded them of their time together, wrote letters that captured their growing feelings, and exchanged virtual hugs that conveyed the warmth of their hearts.

Through every message and call, Elena and Alex navigated the challenges of maintaining a long-distance relationship with grace and determination. They celebrated each other's successes, comforted each other during setbacks, and continued to learn more about each other's strengths and vulnerabilities.

Their love story unfolded through pixels and pixels, proving that distance was no match for the depth of their connection. As their bond continued to evolve digitally, Elena and Alex eagerly looked forward to the next chapter of their journey, knowing that their love was resilient enough to withstand any distance that lay ahead.

Spending Christmas apart was more difficult than either Elena or Alex had anticipated. They had grown accustomed to sharing moments of joy and warmth, but this holiday season, they found themselves separated by miles and time zones.

For Elena, Christmas morning felt bittersweet as she woke up to the familiar sights and sounds of her own home, yet the absence of Alex's presence left an ache in her heart. She missed their tradition of exchanging small, thoughtful gifts and savoring homemade breakfasts together. The twinkling lights and festive decorations seemed dimmer without him by her side.

Alex, too, felt the pang of distance keenly. He missed the warmth of Elena's smile, the way her laughter filled a room, and the comfort of holding her close. The holiday gatherings with friends and family felt incomplete without her, their absence highlighted by the empty space beside him at the dinner table.

Despite the physical separation, Elena and Alex found solace in their digital connection. They exchanged heartfelt messages throughout the day, sharing memories of past holidays and expressing their longing to be together. They reminisced about the moments they had shared in Europe, their laughter echoing across the miles as they recounted their adventures and dreams for the future.

As Christmas Day drew to a close, Elena and Alex found comfort in knowing that their love transcended the physical distance. They cherished the moments they had shared and looked forward to a future when they could create new memories together. Until then, they held onto each other in spirit, finding strength in their enduring bond and the hope of being reunited soon.

After a heartfelt Christmas spent apart, Elena and Alex eagerly anticipated their reunion for New Year's Eve at a picturesque ski mountain. As they drove through winding roads blanketed in snow, anticipation bubbled between them, mingling with the excitement of finally being together again.

Upon arrival, they were greeted by the crisp mountain air and the cheerful bustle of skiers and snowboarders preparing for the evening festivities. Elena and Alex wasted no time in embracing each other warmly, their smiles reflecting the joy of being reunited.

They spent the days leading up to New Year's Eve skiing down snow-covered slopes hand in hand, their laughter echoing through the snowy peaks. In the evenings, they cozied up by the fire, sipping hot cocoa and sharing stories of their time apart. The mountain retreat provided the perfect backdrop for them to reconnect, surrounded by the beauty of nature and the promise of new beginnings.

As the clock ticked closer to midnight on New Year's Eve, Elena and Alex found themselves standing together at the summit, overlooking a breathtaking panorama of stars and snow. They held each other close, feeling the crisp winter air on their faces and the warmth of their love radiating between them.

When the countdown began, they joined the joyful chorus of voices echoing across the mountain, welcoming the new year with hope and excitement. As fireworks illuminated the sky above them, Elena and Alex shared a kiss filled with promise and possibility, knowing that their journey together was just beginning.

In that magical moment, surrounded by the beauty of the ski mountain and the shared anticipation of the future, Elena and Alex felt grateful for the trials that had strengthened their bond and excited for the adventures that lay ahead. Together, they welcomed the new year with hearts full of love, resilience, and the unwavering belief that their love story was destined for greatness.

After their enchanting New Year's celebration on the ski mountain, Elena and Alex returned to their respective cities, their hearts still buzzing with the magic of their time together. It wasn't long before

Elena's friend extended an invitation they couldn't resist: a wedding in Berlin, promising a weekend filled with love, celebration, and a taste of the city's vibrant culture.

Excited to reunite once again, Elena and Alex eagerly accepted the invitation. As they explored Berlin together, they discovered a city pulsating with history and creativity. They wandered through charming neighborhoods, admired the striking architecture, and indulged in culinary delights at local cafes and markets.

Amidst the festivities of the wedding, Elena and Alex found themselves drawn to the city's unconventional and liberating atmosphere. They stumbled upon Berlin's vibrant nightlife scene, where underground clubs and avant-garde performances ignited their senses and awakened a playful, adventurous side of their relationship.

In the midst of this newfound exploration, Elena and Alex discovered a shared openness to new experiences, a willingness to embrace spontaneity, and an unspoken understanding of each other's desires. Their conversations deepened, their laughter echoed through the cobblestone streets, and their touch became imbued with a newfound intimacy.

As they returned to their hotel room after an exhilarating night out, Elena and Alex found themselves sharing whispered secrets and stolen kisses, their connection deepening with each moment of vulnerability and exploration. In Berlin, amidst the celebration of love and the discovery of new horizons, Elena and Alex embraced the kinky side of their relationship, discovering a deeper level of trust, passion, and mutual understanding that would forever enrich their journey together.

Filled with a sense of adventure and a desire to extend their time together, Alex and Elena made a spontaneous decision that would alter their plans dramatically. Instead of parting ways after the wedding in Berlin, Alex suggested that Elena join him in his city, a place she had heard about through his stories but had yet to experience firsthand.

With hearts racing and a sense of anticipation guiding them, they boarded a train that whisked them away from the bustling streets of Berlin to the quieter, more familiar surroundings of Alex's hometown. As they journeyed together, Elena felt a mix of excitement and nerves, unsure of what to expect but trusting in the connection they had forged over their shared adventures.

Arriving in Alex's city, Elena was greeted by the sights and sounds that had shaped his life: the cozy cafes where he spent weekends reading, the parks where he jogged in the mornings, and the charming neighborhoods where he had grown up. Each place carried a piece of Alex's history, offering Elena a deeper understanding of the man she had grown to love.

Throughout their stay, Alex showed Elena his favorite spots, introducing her to his friends and sharing cherished memories from his childhood and youth. They explored museums and art galleries, indulged in local cuisine, and wandered through markets where vendors sold fresh produce and handmade crafts.

In the intimacy of Alex's world, Elena and Alex's relationship blossomed further. They reveled in the simplicity of everyday routines, waking up together to the aroma of freshly brewed coffee and falling asleep beneath a canopy of stars. As they navigated the streets hand in hand, Elena felt a sense of belonging that transcended the excitement of their spontaneous decision.

Their time together in Alex's city became a testament to their growing love and commitment. They embraced the beauty of the ordinary moments and cherished the opportunity to deepen their connection in a place that held significance for both of them. As they prepared to eventually return to their own cities, Elena and Alex carried with them memories of an unforgettable journey that had brought them closer than ever before.

Amidst the bliss of exploring Alex's city together, fate intervened in an unexpected and unforgettable way: a global pandemic struck, disrupting travel and leaving Elena stranded far from her own city. What began as a spontaneous decision to extend their time together now became a test of resilience and love in the face of uncertainty.

As borders closed and travel restrictions tightened, Elena found herself unable to return home. In the midst of a city that was becoming their sanctuary, they faced the reality of navigating through the challenges brought by COVID-19. Together, they adjusted to a new normal—social distancing, wearing masks, and adapting to remote work.

Despite the uncertainties and anxieties that surrounded them, Elena and Alex found solace in each other's company. They supported one another through moments of frustration and fear, finding strength in their shared determination to weather the storm together. Their bond deepened as they spent days exploring the quieter corners of the city, discovering hidden parks and cozy bookshops that offered moments of peace amidst the chaos.

As the weeks turned into months, their love grew stronger amidst the backdrop of uncertainty. They found joy in simple pleasures—cooking meals together, binge-watching movies, and having deep conversations that spanned from the mundane to the profound. Elena marveled at Alex's unwavering support and kindness, while Alex found comfort in Elena's resilience and optimism.

In the face of adversity, Elena and Alex discovered the true meaning of partnership and commitment. They celebrated milestones virtually with loved ones, leaned on each other during moments of doubt, and found hope in the promise of a future where they could once again travel freely and without fear. Despite the unexpected turn of events, they knew that their journey through the pandemic had only strengthened their love, preparing them for the challenges and joys that lay ahead.

As the months passed and they navigated the uncertainties of the pandemic together, Elena and Alex found themselves contemplating a new chapter in their relationship: moving in together. What began as a spontaneous decision to extend Elena's stay in Alex's city had blossomed into a deep partnership grounded in love, trust, and mutual support.

Their days were filled with shared laughter, quiet moments of reflection, and the comfort of knowing they could rely on each other through thick and thin. They had grown accustomed to waking up to the sight of each other, sharing meals, and creating a home together amidst the challenges of the pandemic.

One evening, as they sat by the window watching the city lights twinkle below, Alex turned to Elena with a gentle smile. He spoke of their journey together—the highs and lows, the adventures and uncertainties—and expressed his desire to take the next step in their relationship. Elena listened intently, her heart swelling with love as Alex shared his vision of a future where they could wake up together every day, build a life, and face whatever challenges came their way as a team.

Moved by Alex's words and the depth of their connection, Elena felt a surge of warmth and certainty. She took his hands in hers and shared her dreams of a shared future filled with love, laughter, and endless possibilities. In that quiet moment, amidst the backdrop of a city that had become their refuge, they made a heartfelt commitment to move in together—a decision rooted in love, strengthened by their journey through the pandemic, and imbued with hope for a bright and joyful future.

With plans in motion and hearts full of excitement, Elena and Alex eagerly began searching for a place they could call their own—a sanctuary where their love could continue to grow and flourish. They embraced the challenges and joys of setting up their new home, knowing that every step they took together was a testament to the strength of their bond and the enduring power of their love story.

As Elena and Alex embarked on their journey of moving in together, they found themselves drawn not only to a shared physical space but also to the process of creating a home that reflected their love and aspirations. After carefully considering their options, they took a bold step forward and decided to purchase a place together—a decision that symbolized their commitment and dedication to building a future side by side.

With excitement and anticipation, Alex took on the role of the ultimate romantic, showering Elena with gestures of love that extended beyond mere material possessions. He meticulously curated their new home, selecting furniture that blended their tastes into a harmonious whole. From cozy rugs that softened the floors to artwork that spoke to their shared passions, every corner of their space bore the imprint of their journey together.

Alex's thoughtful gestures extended beyond the aesthetic realm. He surprised Elena with meaningful gifts—a vintage record player to serenade their evenings, a collection of books by her favourite authors, and a cozy reading nook where they could unwind together after a long day. Each gift was a testament to his deep understanding of Elena's heart and a reflection of his desire to create a space where they could thrive as a couple.

Beyond the material aspects, their journey of setting up their home became a labour of love—a shared adventure marked by laughter, compromise, and the joy of building a life together. They navigated the intricacies of blending their belongings, creating rituals that honoured their identities while forging a unified path forward.

As they settled into their new home, Elena and Alex found themselves surrounded not only by possessions but also by a sense of belonging and shared dreams. Their commitment to each other deepened with each passing day, grounded in the foundation they had laid together—a sanctuary where their love could continue to grow, nurtured by the memories they created and the future they envisioned side by side.

Chapter 3: The Discovery

As Elena and Alex settled into their new home and deepened their commitment to each other, Elena began to notice subtle shifts in Alex's behaviour that sparked a sense of unease. At first, it was small things—missed calls that he couldn't quite explain, secretive conversations that trailed off when she entered the room, and unexplained absences that left her questioning his whereabouts.

Despite her initial reluctance to entertain doubts, these signs of deceit began to accumulate, casting a shadow over their once-secure relationship. Elena wrestled with conflicting emotions—she trusted Alex deeply yet couldn't shake the growing sense that something was amiss. She longed for reassurance, hoping that her suspicions were unfounded and that their love could weather any storm.

As weeks passed, Alex's behaviour became increasingly erratic. He grew defensive when Elena gently probed for answers, dismissing her concerns with vague explanations and promises to do better. His once-open demeanour now seemed guarded, leaving Elena to wonder if there were aspects of his life that he was keeping hidden from her.

Caught between love and doubt, Elena found herself scrutinizing their interactions, searching for clues to understand the truth behind Alex's actions. She yearned for the openness and honesty that had defined their early days together, grappling with the painful realization that their relationship might be facing a crisis she never anticipated.

In moments of solitude, Elena questioned her instincts, grappling with the fear of confronting a reality that threatened to unravel the future they had envisioned. She clung to memories of their shared moments and the deep connection they had forged, desperately hoping that they could navigate this tumultuous chapter and emerge stronger on the other side.

As uncertainty loomed over their once-bright horizon, Elena faced a daunting choice—confront the signs of deceit and seek clarity, or retreat into the safety of denial and risk losing herself in the process. Whatever path she chose, one thing remained certain: their journey together had reached a crossroads where trust, truth, and resilience would ultimately define the fate of their love.

Elena's doubts about Alex grew when she noticed a name recurring in his phone conversations: Maria, a dental nurse from Mexico. He mentioned her casually at first, speaking of her struggles and his efforts to help her secure a visa.

"She's just someone I'm helping out," he explained one evening, brushing off her questions with a laugh.

But Elena couldn't shake the feeling that there was more to the story. His phone buzzed late into the night, and when she glanced at the screen, her stomach tightened at the sight of Maria's name.

"Why is she texting you so late?" Elena asked, trying to keep her voice steady.

Alex sighed, placing his phone face down on the table. "She's going through a lot right now. I told you—I'm just being supportive. You know how much I care about helping people."

Elena nodded, but the explanation felt too neat, too practiced. That night, as Alex slept, she wrestled with her unease. Part of her felt guilty for doubting him, but another part—the part that noticed the way he avoided direct answers—refused to dismiss her instincts.

The following day, Elena decided to check his phone. Her hands trembled as she scrolled through his messages. What she found made her blood run cold: a string of affectionate texts and photos exchanged over months.

When she confronted Alex, he looked at her with a mix of anger and disbelief. "You went through my phone?" he spat. "Do you even trust me? This is why relationships fail—because people like you can't respect boundaries."

Elena stood her ground, her voice trembling but firm. "Boundaries? You've been lying to me, Alex. I deserve the truth."

He ran a hand through his hair, his expression softening. "Fine. Maybe I crossed a line by getting too close to her. But it's harmless, Elena. She means nothing to me compared to you."

But the cracks were already too wide to repair with reassurances. Elena realized that their relationship, once built on trust, was crumbling under the weight of secrets.

Initially, Alex shared heartwarming stories about his desire to support individuals in need, portraying himself as compassionate and altruistic. However, as Elena probed further into his involvement, discrepancies emerged. Alex's explanations about his communications with the nurse seemed vague and evasive, and when pressed for details, he became defensive and dismissive. She noticed discrepancies in his timeline and observed inconsistencies in his explanations, which raised red flags and ignited a sense of betrayal.

Elena struggled with conflicting emotions—she wanted to trust Alex, yet the evidence of deceit gnawed at her. She confronted him with her findings, hoping for transparency and honesty, but instead, his responses were muddled and lacked clarity. His attempts to justify his actions only deepened Elena's sense of disillusionment and hurt.

As Elena grappled with the painful realization that Alex may have misrepresented his intentions, she faced a pivotal moment of reckoning in their relationship. She questioned the authenticity of their connection and wondered if she truly knew the person she had committed her heart to. The foundation of trust they had painstakingly built seemed shaken, and Elena found herself grappling with the daunting choice of whether to confront Alex directly or withdraw to protect herself from further disappointment.

Amid the uncertainty, Elena held onto a glimmer of hope that they could confront this challenge together and emerge stronger. Yet, she knew that their journey forward would require honesty, vulnerability, and a willingness to confront uncomfortable truths. As she navigated the complexities of love and betrayal, Elena understood that the path ahead would demand courage and resilience, whatever the outcome might be.

As Elena delved deeper into understanding Alex's behaviours, she began to notice a troubling pattern: his tendency to seek validation from his ex-partners and other women. Initially, Alex had portrayed himself as confident and self-assured, but as their relationship progressed, Elena became aware of his lingering connections with past flames.

She discovered subtle signs of ongoing communication—innocuous messages that seemed harmless at first glance but hinted at a deeper emotional attachment. Alex's interactions with these women often centred around seeking affirmation and validation, whether through casual compliments or nostalgic reminiscences of shared memories.

Elena's heart sank as she realized the extent of Alex's need for external validation. She wrestled with feelings of inadequacy and insecurity, questioning whether she could ever measure up to the standards set by these past relationships. The realization left her feeling vulnerable and uncertain about the foundation of their relationship.

Confronting Alex about her discoveries proved challenging. He initially downplayed the significance of his interactions, dismissing them as harmless gestures of friendship. However, as Elena pressed for transparency and honesty, Alex's defensiveness grew, revealing a deeper discomfort with addressing his emotional dependencies on others.

As Elena navigated the complexities of love and trust, she grappled with the difficult choice of whether to accept Alex's explanations and continue their journey together or confront the underlying issues that threatened to undermine their relationship. She yearned for a resolution that would restore the trust they had built and reaffirm the authenticity of their connection.

In the midst of uncertainty, Elena recognized the importance of asserting her worth and boundaries. She sought clarity in understanding Alex's motivations and intentions, hoping for a future where their love could be grounded in mutual respect, honesty, and a commitment to building a healthy, fulfilling partnership.

As Elena navigated the complexities of her relationship with Alex, she found herself confronted with another layer of challenge: Alex's mounting business troubles. What had once been a source of stability and success now became a source of stress and uncertainty, casting a shadow over their lives together.

Alex had always been driven and ambitious, pouring his energy into his career with a passion that Elena admired. However, as economic challenges and unforeseen setbacks emerged, his once-thriving business began to falter. The pressures of financial strain weighed heavily on him, affecting his mood and demeanour.

Elena witnessed firsthand the toll that these troubles took on Alex. He became preoccupied with work, often withdrawing into silence or burying himself in endless hours of strategizing and planning. The stress began to seep into their relationship, overshadowing their moments of joy and intimacy with a cloud of worry and uncertainty.

Despite her concerns, Elena remained steadfast by Alex's side, offering him unwavering support and encouragement. She listened patiently as he shared his fears and frustrations, offering a reassuring presence in moments of doubt. Together, they navigated the challenges as a team, seeking solutions and making difficult decisions with determination and resilience.

As they faced each obstacle together, Elena's admiration for Alex's strength and resilience grew. She witnessed his unwavering commitment to overcoming adversity, even in the face of daunting odds. Their relationship evolved as they leaned on each other for emotional support, finding solace in the shared journey of navigating through turbulent times.

Through it all, Elena remained hopeful that their love would weather the storm of Alex's business troubles. She believed in his ability to rise above the challenges, knowing that their bond had been forged through moments of both joy and hardship. Together, they confronted the uncertainties of the future with courage and determination, holding onto the belief that their love story was resilient enough to withstand any storm that life threw their way.

Elena's growing suspicions about Alex's involvement with the Mexican dental nurse reached a breaking point one evening as she sat alone in their cozy living room, her mind racing with unanswered questions and a sense of unease that refused to be ignored. Despite Alex's reassurances and attempts to downplay the situation, Elena's intuition told her that there was more to the story than he was willing to admit.

Unable to shake off her doubts, Elena made a difficult decision to investigate further. With a heavy heart and a knot of anxiety in her stomach, she quietly began to piece together clues—tracking phone records, sifting through emails, and meticulously revisiting conversations that had raised red flags in her mind.

As she delved deeper into her investigation, Elena uncovered unsettling truths that shattered her illusions of trust and security. She discovered clandestine messages exchanged between Alex and the Mexican girl, revealing a level of emotional intimacy that went beyond what he had disclosed. The details painted a picture of deceit and betrayal that left Elena reeling with disbelief and heartache.

Confronted with irrefutable evidence, Elena confronted Alex with a mix of anger, hurt, and disappointment. She demanded honesty and accountability, refusing to accept half-truths or attempts to justify his actions. Alex, caught off guard by Elena's findings, struggled to explain himself, his excuses falling short in the face of her righteous indignation.

In the aftermath of their confrontation, Elena wrestled with conflicting emotions—anguish over the betrayal she had uncovered, a sense of betrayal, and a deep sadness over the shattered trust that had once defined their relationship. She faced a daunting choice: whether to salvage what remained of their bond or walk away from the wreckage of their love story, knowing that the wounds inflicted would take time to heal.

Amidst the pain and turmoil, Elena found solace in the support of loved ones who rallied around her with words of comfort and empathy. She leaned on their strength as she navigated the tumultuous aftermath of her discovery, grappling with the profound loss of the future she had envisioned with Alex and the painful journey of rebuilding her sense of self-worth and trust in others.

As Elena confronted Alex with her findings about his interactions with the Mexican girl, she expected honesty and accountability. Instead, Alex's reaction shocked her to the core. He vehemently denied any wrongdoing, accusing Elena of invading his privacy and fabricating false accusations. His words cut deep, leaving Elena feeling confused, gaslit, and emotionally drained.

Alex's gaslighting tactics only intensified Elena's anxiety and distress. He minimized her concerns, dismissed her evidence as misinterpretations, and manipulated her into questioning her sanity. He portrayed himself as the victim, casting doubt on Elena's motives and undermining her sense of reality.

Unable to sleep, Elena tossed and turned, replaying their confrontations and grappling with the weight of betrayal and deceit.

Her mind raced with unanswered questions and conflicting emotions, torn between wanting to believe in the love they had shared and the painful truths she had uncovered.

As days turned into sleepless nights, Elena found herself consumed by a turbulent mix of anger, hurt, and disbelief. She struggled to reconcile the person she thought Alex was with the one she now saw—a man capable of deception and manipulation. Her anxiety deepened as she navigated the aftermath of confronting Alex, wrestling with the profound sense of loss and betrayal that threatened to engulf her.

In moments of solitude, Elena sought refuge in the support of trusted friends and family who validated her feelings and offered a lifeline of empathy and understanding. Their unwavering presence provided a beacon of hope amidst the storm, reminding Elena that she was not alone in her pain and that healing would come with time and self-compassion.

As Elena confronted the harsh reality of Alex's gaslighting and emotional manipulation, she vowed to prioritize her well-being and rebuild her sense of trust and self-worth. She faced a long road ahead, but she knew that reclaiming her strength and resilience would ultimately lead her to a place of healing and newfound clarity.

Elena then discovered that he had relationships with one of the staff he hired who still works for him, and he even blamed Elena for trying to cripple his business as she asked him to move that stuff out. And it didn't just end there then another lady he hired but somehow didn't stay on and other lawsuits involving female employees whom he had some relationships with. Alex's been sending money to many other female friends that he claims he is helping, but it is just an array of them.

Who is Alex?

In the professional sphere, Alex's charismatic facade often masked a darker reality—a tendency to treat business partners and colleagues with callousness and indifference. His ambitious drive and desire for success were tempered by a ruthless streak that left a trail of burned bridges in his wake.

Elena witnessed firsthand the repercussions of Alex's behaviour in business dealings. He wielded his authority with an iron fist, often prioritizing short-term gains over long-term relationships. His decisions were marked by a lack of empathy and a willingness to sacrifice integrity for personal gain, leaving collaborators and colleagues feeling exploited and disregarded.

Behind closed doors, Elena observed tense negotiations that often escalated into confrontational standoffs. Alex's disregard for compromise and his insistence on dominating every interaction alienated potential allies and strained existing partnerships. His reputation as a formidable but unforgiving business partner spread quickly, casting a shadow over his professional endeavours.

Despite Elena's attempts to counsel moderation and empathy, Alex remained steadfast in his approach—a belief that success justified any means necessary. His actions bred resentment and mistrust among peers, further isolating him in a competitive world where collaboration and mutual respect were key to sustainable growth.

As Elena navigated the complexities of their relationship, she struggled to reconcile the charismatic man she loved with the ruthless businessman she witnessed in action. She questioned the ethics of his decisions and the implications for their shared future, grappling with the moral dilemmas posed by Alex's uncompromising pursuit of success.

In moments of introspection, Elena confronted the harsh reality of Alex's behaviour—a stark contrast to the values she held dear. She faced difficult conversations about the impact of his actions on their relationship and the broader consequences for their personal and professional lives.

As their journey together unfolded, Elena found herself at a crossroads of loyalty and self-preservation. She confronted the difficult truth that love alone could not erase the ethical divides that separated them. With each passing day, she navigated the delicate balance of supporting Alex while safeguarding her own principles and aspirations for a future built on integrity and mutual respect.

Through it all, Elena remained hopeful that Alex would recognize the toll of his actions and embrace a path of growth and reconciliation. She believed in his capacity for change and the possibility of forging a partnership grounded in shared values and a commitment to ethical conduct. As they confronted the challenges of their intertwined lives, Elena held onto the hope that their love could transcend the shadows of Alex's past decisions, paving the way for a future where integrity and compassion would guide their journey forward.

Alex's business dealings were fraught with turbulence, marked by a series of lawsuits that underscored the contentious nature of his professional interactions. From disputes with suppliers over contract terms and payment delays to legal battles with competitors over intellectual property rights, Alex found himself embroiled in a web of litigation that strained his resources and tarnished his reputation.

Elena witnessed the mounting stress and emotional toll that each lawsuit took on Alex. His once-confident demeanour faltered under the weight of legal challenges, forcing him to navigate complex negotiations and courtroom dramas that threatened to unravel years of hard work and ambition.

The lawsuits extended beyond external conflicts to include internal strife as well. Alex's business decisions often clashed with the expectations of his staff and even his brother, leading to bitter disputes over management practices and financial accountability. These internal rifts further exacerbated the strain on Alex's relationships and tested his ability to lead with integrity and empathy.

Despite Elena's unwavering support, she struggled to reconcile the ethical dilemmas posed by Alex's legal battles. She grappled with questions about the impact of his actions on their future together and the broader implications for their personal and professional lives. Each lawsuit brought renewed uncertainty and introspection, prompting difficult conversations about values, priorities, and the boundaries of loyalty.

As they navigated the stormy waters of legal challenges and professional strife, Elena remained by Alex's side, offering a steady anchor of emotional support and guidance. Together, they confronted the consequences of his decisions and sought to chart a path forward that honoured their shared values and aspirations for a harmonious future.

Through the turmoil, Elena held onto the belief that Alex's resilience and determination would ultimately guide them through the darkest moments. She hoped for a resolution that would not only restore his professional standing but also reaffirm their commitment to building a life together based on trust, integrity, and mutual respect. As they faced the uncertainties of their intertwined lives, Elena found solace in the strength of their love and the possibility of forging a future where their shared journey could overcome the shadows of legal challenges and pave the way for a brighter tomorrow.

Elena's journey with Alex took an unexpected turn as she uncovered unsettling truths about his business practices. What began as concerns over his professional demeanour and legal battles escalated when she stumbled upon evidence suggesting Alex had misappropriated funds within his company.

At first, Elena noticed discrepancies in their financial records—unexplained expenses, irregularities in revenue reporting, and payments made to unfamiliar entities. As she delved deeper, she unearthed a trail of transactions that pointed to Alex diverting company funds for personal use, a revelation that shook her to the core.

Confronting Alex about her discoveries proved emotionally charged and tumultuous. He initially denied any wrongdoing, dismissing Elena's concerns as misunderstandings or misinterpretations of the financial complexities involved in running a business. His deflections and justifications only fueled Elena's determination to uncover the truth, driven by a deep-seated need for transparency and accountability.

As the magnitude of Alex's actions became clearer, Elena grappled with conflicting emotions—betrayal over his breach of trust, disbelief at the extent of his deception, and a profound sense of uncertainty about their future together. The implications of his misappropriation of funds extended beyond financial loss, casting doubt on the foundation of their relationship and challenging her beliefs about his integrity.

In the aftermath of their confrontations, Elena faced difficult decisions about her role in Alex's life and the consequences of his actions. She wrestled with the ethical implications of his behaviour and the impact on their shared dreams and aspirations. Each day brought new revelations and painful realizations, prompting introspection about the boundaries of loyalty and the limits of forgiveness.

Amidst the turmoil, Elena sought solace in the support of loved ones who offered a refuge of empathy and understanding. Their unwavering presence provided a source of strength as she navigated the complexities of love and betrayal, grappling with the daunting choice of whether to stand by Alex during his darkest hour or prioritize her well-being and seek a path of healing.

Through it all, Elena confronted the harsh realities of Alex's misappropriation of funds with courage and resilience. She embarked on a journey of self-discovery and healing, determined to reclaim her sense of identity and rebuild her trust in relationships. As she navigated the uncertain terrain ahead, Elena held onto the hope that honesty and integrity would ultimately guide her toward a future where love could be forged from the ashes of betrayal and where she could find peace and fulfillment on her terms.

Elena's world turned upside down when she discovered that Alex had been using the company's funds to support his lavish lifestyle. What had initially seemed like minor discrepancies in their financial records gradually unravelled into a disturbing pattern of financial misconduct?

It started with extravagant purchases and indulgent trips that seemed beyond the scope of their business operations. Elena noticed discrepancies in expense reports, unauthorized withdrawals from company accounts, and payments made to obscure vendors that raised red flags. As she dug deeper, she uncovered a web of transactions that pointed to Alex diverting significant sums of money for personal expenses.

Confronting Alex about her findings was emotionally charged, and she met with vehement denial. He initially dismissed Elena's concerns as misunderstandings or necessary expenses for business development. His attempts to justify his actions fell flat in the face of overwhelming evidence, leaving Elena grappling with a profound sense of betrayal and disbelief.

The implications of Alex's misuse of company funds were profound. It jeopardized the financial stability of their business, strained relationships with stakeholders and investors, and undermined the trust of employees who relied on the company's integrity. Elena struggled with the ethical dilemma of standing by Alex during his darkest hour or prioritizing the well-being of those affected by his actions.

As Elena navigated the aftermath of her discoveries, she faced difficult decisions about her future with Alex and the consequences of his behaviour. She confronted the ethical boundaries of loyalty and forgiveness, wrestling with the painful realization that their dreams and aspirations had been built on shaky foundations.

Amidst the chaos, Elena sought solace in the support of loved ones who offered a sanctuary of empathy and understanding. Their unwavering presence provided a source of strength as she navigated the complexities of love and betrayal, determined to reclaim her sense of identity and rebuild her trust in relationships.

Amid the uncertainty, Elena held onto the hope that transparency and accountability would ultimately guide her toward a future where honesty and integrity could restore her faith in love and pave the way for a life where she could find peace and fulfillment on her terms.

Chapter 4: Control

As their relationship progressed, Alex's influence over Elena grew. He insisted on knowing her every move, disguised as concern for her well-being. He began to isolate her from friends and family, subtly undermining her confidence and independence. He was the go-to person for anything and everything "You don't need them," he would say, his voice soothing yet insistent. "They don't understand you like I do."

Elena found herself agreeing, even as a part of her resistance. She wanted to believe in the image Alex projected, the perfect partner who loved her unconditionally. But the cracks in his façade were becoming harder to ignore.

As their relationship progressed, Alex's influence over Elena grew more pervasive. What had once seemed like genuine concern for her well-being gradually revealed itself as a means of control. He insisted on knowing her every move, his inquiries masked as loving attentiveness. "I just want to make sure you're safe," he would say, his tone gentle yet firm.

Subtlety became Alex's weapon of choice in his campaign to isolate Elena from her support network. He began to subtly undermine her confidence and independence, planting seeds of doubt about her relationships with friends and family. "They don't understand you as I do," he would assert, his voice soothing yet insistent. "You don't need them."

At first, Elena found herself agreeing, drawn to the image Alex projected—the perfect partner who loved her unconditionally. She began to rely on him for everything, seeing him as her rock in an increasingly turbulent world. He became her go-to person for advice, support, and even minor decisions, gradually eroding her autonomy.

However, the cracks in Alex's façade were becoming harder to ignore. Elena noticed the subtle ways he manipulated her thoughts and feelings, his concern often crossing the line into control. He discouraged her from attending social gatherings, subtly suggesting that her friends were a bad influence. Family visits became rare, as Alex always seemed to find reasons why she should stay with him instead.

Elena's world grew smaller, her once vibrant social circle shrinking as she leaned more heavily on Alex. She wanted to believe in his unwavering love and support, but a part of her resisted. She felt the creeping sense of isolation, the loss of her own voice amidst Alex's overwhelming presence.

Friends and family tried to reach out, their concern growing as they noticed Elena's increasing withdrawal. Yet, Alex's influence was strong, his reassurances convincing. He painted a picture of a world where only he truly understood and cared for her, a world where anyone outside their bubble was a potential threat to their happiness.

Despite her internal struggle, Elena began to see glimpses of the reality beneath Alex's charming exterior. The more he sought to control her, the more she questioned the foundation of their relationship. She longed for the independence and confidence she once had, recognizing the subtle chains that bound her to Alex's manipulative influence.

As Elena grappled with her feelings, she faced the daunting challenge of reclaiming her sense of self and breaking free from the subtle but suffocating grip of Alex's control. It was a journey fraught with emotional turmoil and uncertainty, but one she knew she had to undertake to rediscover her own strength and independence.

Elena's life had undergone a dramatic transformation since meeting Alex. As their relationship deepened, she made the monumental decision to move her entire family to Alex's city. It was a leap of faith, driven by love and the desire to build a future together. Alex's charm and promises of a better life convinced Elena that this was the right choice. He painted a vivid picture of a perfect life together, a blend of romance and stability that seemed too good to pass up.

The move was a logistical challenge, but Alex's reassurances eased Elena's concerns. "We'll be happier here," he told her, his voice filled with confidence and warmth. "Your family will thrive, and we'll be closer than ever." Elena wanted to believe him, to trust in the dream he was selling.

Settling into the new city, Elena initially felt optimistic. Alex helped her family find a suitable home and even assisted with their transition, making sure everything went smoothly. For a while, it seemed like the move was a success. Her parents appreciated Alex's generosity, and her siblings found new opportunities in the bustling metropolis.

However, as time went on, Alex's controlling behavior became more pronounced. He began to dictate not only Elena's life but also the lives of her family members. Decisions about schooling for her children, healthcare for her parents, and even social activities were now filtered through Alex's preferences. "I just want what's best for all of you," he would say, but his actions suggested otherwise.

Elena noticed how Alex subtly discouraged her family from maintaining their old connections. He made it inconvenient for them to visit their friends back home, always finding reasons to keep them in the city. "You have everything you need right here," he insisted. Slowly, her family's world shrank to the confines of Alex's influence.

The isolation took its toll. Elena's family began to sense the underlying tension, but they were reluctant to speak up. They saw the strain in Elena's eyes, the way she hesitated before agreeing with Alex's suggestions. Yet, they were caught in a delicate balance—grateful for his help but wary of his overreach.

Despite the veneer of a perfect life, cracks were starting to appear. Elena's parents voiced their concerns gently, urging her to reconsider the extent of Alex's control. Her parents expressed frustration at their newfound restrictions, missing the freedom they once had. Elena felt torn between her love for her family and the overpowering influence of Alex.

As Alex's grip tightened, Elena's internal struggle grew more intense. She realized that moving her family to his city had woven them deeper into his web of control. The dream that once seemed so promising was now a gilded cage, trapping her and her loved ones in a life dictated by Alex's whims.

Determined to regain control, Elena began to seek ways to reconnect with her own voice and independence. She reached out to old friends, rekindling relationships that Alex had tried to sever. Slowly, she started to rebuild her support network, finding strength in the connections she had nearly lost.

Elena's journey was far from over, but she knew one thing for certain: she had to reclaim her life, not just for herself but for her family as well. The path to freedom and self-discovery was fraught with challenges, but with each step, Elena grew more resilient, ready to face whatever lay ahead with newfound courage and determination.

As the weight of Alex's control became more unbearable, Elena made a bold decision to reclaim her independence. She started searching for a job, determined to set herself free from the suffocating grip of Alex's influence. This decision marked a turning point in her life, a step toward reclaiming her autonomy and rediscovering her own strength.

Elena's search was not easy. Alex had subtly discouraged her from pursuing a career, insisting that her focus should be on their relationship and managing their household. "You don't need to work," he would say, masking his control as concern. But Elena knew that finding a job was essential for her mental and emotional well-being.

After months of searching, Elena finally found a position at an international technology consulting firm. The job was demanding but invigorating, offering her a sense of purpose and a space where she could express her creativity. Her new role required long hours and dedication, but the rewards were immediate—a paycheck that represented her financial independence and colleagues who valued her skills and input.

Each day at work, Elena felt a little more like herself. The office environment was a stark contrast to the confines of her life with Alex. Her coworkers respected her opinions, and her contributions were acknowledged and appreciated. For the first time in a long while, Elena felt empowered and confident in her abilities.

As Elena's confidence grew, so did her determination to regain control of her life. She began to set boundaries with Alex, asserting her independence and making it clear that she was no longer willing to be controlled. "I have a job now, Alex," she told him one evening, her voice steady. "I need to focus on my career and my well-being."

Alex reacted with a mix of disbelief and anger. "You don't need to work, Elena. I can provide for us," he insisted, his tone growing more desperate. But Elena stood her ground, her newfound sense of self-worth bolstering her resolve. "This is important to me, Alex. I need to do this for myself."

The tension between them grew, but Elena's job became her sanctuary. It provided her with the stability and strength she needed to confront Alex's manipulative behavior. She began to see through his attempts to undermine her confidence and recognized his tactics for what they were—a means of keeping her dependent and isolated.

With each passing day, Elena's independence flourished. She reconnected with friends and family, rebuilding the relationships that Alex had tried to sever. Her family, seeing her newfound strength, rallied around her, offering their unwavering support. They understood the importance of her journey and stood by her as she navigated the challenges of breaking free from Alex's control.

Elena's job became more than just a means to an end; it was a symbol of her resilience and determination. It marked the beginning of a new chapter in her life, one where she could rediscover her identity and live on her own terms. As she looked toward the future, Elena felt a renewed sense of hope and possibility, ready to embrace whatever came next with courage and conviction.

When Alex discovered that Elena had found a job, his reaction was swift and cruel. The man who had once showered her with affection and promises of a perfect life now turned on her with a ferocity she hadn't anticipated. His supportive facade crumbled, revealing a vindictive and manipulative side that left Elena reeling.

"What were you thinking?" Alex spat, his voice laced with contempt. "You don't need to work for others but focus on building the business that we have. I provide everything for you!" The words stung each one a dagger aimed at undermining her newfound sense of independence.

Elena stood her ground, her heart pounding in her chest. "I need this, Alex. I need to feel useful and independent. I need to do this for myself."

But Alex was relentless. He discarded her emotionally, turning cold and distant. He refused to acknowledge her accomplishments or the importance of her job. Instead, he shamed her, making snide remarks about her capabilities and belittling her ambitions.

"You think you're so important now because you have a job," he sneered one evening. "But you're nothing without me. Your little job means nothing in the grand scheme of things."

His words cut deep, but Elena refused to let them break her spirit. She had come too far to let Alex's cruelty drag her back into a life of dependence and control. She sought solace in her work, where she found validation and respect that Alex had never truly given her.

In the days that followed, Alex's behavior grew more erratic and hostile. He would pick fights over trivial matters, using every opportunity to undermine her confidence and assert his dominance. He tried to isolate her further, cutting off her contact with friends and family, and criticizing her for spending time away from home.

Despite the emotional turmoil, Elena's resolve only strengthened. She leaned on her colleagues for support, finding allies who understood her struggles and offered a safe space where she could share her experiences. Her family, too, rallied around her, their concern turning into steadfast support as they witnessed Alex's true nature.

Elena's job became her refuge, a place where she could escape the toxicity of her relationship and focus on building a future for herself. The more Alex tried to tear her down, the more determined she became to rise above his attempts to control and demean her.

One evening, after yet another vicious argument, Elena realized that she could no longer stay with Alex. His relentless shaming and attempts to undermine her autonomy had crossed a line she couldn't ignore. With a heavy heart but a clear mind, she made the decision to leave.

Elena packed her bags, each item a testament to her reclaiming her life. As she walked out the door, she felt a mixture of fear and liberation. Fear of the unknown and the challenges that lay ahead, but also liberation from the oppressive weight of Alex's control.

In the days and weeks that followed, Elena embraced her independence with a renewed sense of purpose. She continued to thrive at her job, drawing strength from her achievements and the supportive network she had built. She reconnected with friends and family, finding joy in the relationships that had been strained by Alex's manipulation.

Elena's journey was far from over, but she faced it with courage and resilience. She had broken free from Alex's grasp, reclaiming her autonomy and rediscovering her own strength. As she looked toward the future, she knew that she could overcome any challenge, armed with the knowledge that she was worthy of respect, love, and independence.

After the initial shock of Elena leaving, Alex's anger morphed into desperation. He couldn't believe that she had the strength to walk away from him. Realizing the depth of his loss, he swallowed his pride and reached out to her, begging her to come back.

"Elena, please," Alex's voice trembled over the phone. "I'm sorry for everything. I didn't mean those things I said. I need you. We can work this out. Please come home."

Elena felt a pang of sorrow hearing his plea. Despite everything, a part of her still remembered the man she had fallen in love with, the man who had once made her feel special and cherished. But the pain of his recent actions was too fresh, his betrayal too profound to simply forget.

"Alex, it's not that simple," she replied, her voice steady but filled with emotion. "You hurt me deeply. You controlled me, belittled me, and tried to make me dependent on you. I can't just go back to that."

Alex's desperation grew. He promised to change, to be better, to respect her independence. He assured her that he understood his mistakes and that he was willing to do whatever it took to make things right. "Elena, please give me another chance. I can't imagine my life without you."

Elena hesitated. The sincerity in Alex's voice was palpable, but so was the memory of his manipulative behavior. She knew that actions spoke louder than words and that Alex had a long way to go to prove that he could truly change.

"I need time, Alex," she said finally. "Time to think, time to heal. I can't promise anything right now, but I need you to respect my decision."

Days turned into weeks, and Alex's attempts to win her back became more intense. He sent flowers, heartfelt letters, and messages filled with remorse and promises of a better future. He showed up at her workplace, pleading for a chance to talk, to make amends.

Elena, however, remained resolute. She appreciated his efforts but knew that true change required more than just words and gestures. It required a fundamental shift in his attitude and behavior, something that couldn't happen overnight.

As she navigated her new life, Elena found strength in her independence and the support of her friends, family, and colleagues. She continued to excel at her job, drawing confidence from her achievements and the respect she earned from those around her.

Alex's pleas slowly began to wane, replaced by a sombre acceptance, Elena felt bad, and she decided to ask him for a meeting. Alex and Elena met to discuss their arguments. During their conversation, they carefully listened to each other's perspectives and concerns. By acknowledging the validity of each other's points and communicating openly, they managed to find common ground. Ultimately, they reached an agreement that satisfied both parties. Their discussion not only resolved the immediate issues but also strengthened their mutual understanding and respect. Elena agreed to return home and she thought this was the turning point and everything was going to be alright.

Alex realized that he needed to reflect on his actions and truly understand the damage he had caused. For the first time, he has the thought to seek professional help, hoping to confront the issues that had led to his controlling behaviour.

Elena, meanwhile, focused on her personal growth and healing. She embraced new opportunities, rediscovered her passions, and built a life that reflected her true self. While the memories of her time with Alex lingered, they served as a reminder of her strength and resilience.

In the end, Elena knew that her journey was one of self-discovery and empowerment. Whether or not Alex could genuinely change was no longer her responsibility but his. She kept reminding herself that she had found her own path, one that led to a future filled with hope, independence, and the promise of a life lived on her own terms and not to live the life that he wants her to live but she kept walking back into the trap, not even noticing.

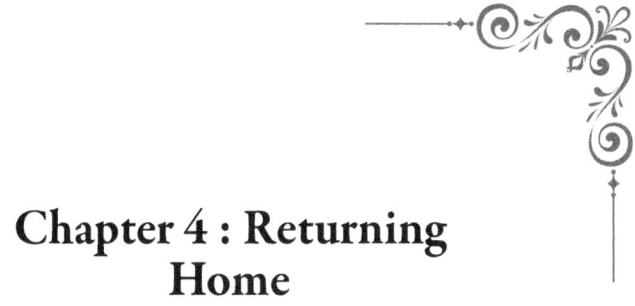

Chapter 4 : Returning Home

After many discussions and promises, Elena came to a difficult decision. Despite her reservations, she decided to give Alex one last chance and return home. His persistent apologies and heartfelt vows to change finally wore down her defenses. She hoped that he had truly understood the depth of his mistakes and was sincere about wanting to build a healthier relationship.

The day Elena returned, Alex greeted her with a mixture of relief and trepidation. He had prepared their home meticulously, ensuring everything was perfect for her arrival. Flowers adorned the living room, and her favorite meal was ready on the dining table. "Welcome home, Elena," he said softly, his eyes filled with a blend of hope and gratitude.

Elena stepped inside, feeling a mixture of emotions. The home that once felt like a gilded cage now seemed different. She had changed, and she hoped Alex had too. "Thank you, Alex," she replied, managing a small smile. "Let's take things one step at a time."

In the following weeks, Alex worked hard to prove his commitment to change. He sought therapy and joined support groups to address his controlling behavior. He made a conscious effort to respect Elena's independence, giving her the space she needed and encouraging her pursuits.

Elena, in turn, approached their renewed relationship with cautious optimism. She set clear boundaries and communicated her needs openly, making it clear that she would not tolerate any attempts to control or belittle her. "This has to be different, Alex," she emphasized during one of their many heart-to-heart talks. "I need to know that you respect me as an equal partner."

Alex nodded, his expression earnest. "I understand, Elena. I want to be the partner you deserve. I know it will take time, but I am committed to making this work."

Gradually, they found a new rhythm. Alex attended Elena's work functions, showing genuine interest in her career and celebrating her successes. He also made an effort to rebuild bridges with her family, seeking their forgiveness and understanding. His actions spoke louder than words, and Elena began to see glimpses of the man she had once loved.

Despite these positive changes, there were moments of doubt and fear. Elena remained vigilant, watching for any signs of Alex slipping back into his old patterns. Trust was not something that could be rebuilt overnight, and she needed time to fully believe in his transformation.

As they navigated this new phase of their relationship, Elena also focused on her own growth. She continued to excel at her job, finding fulfillment and confidence in her achievements. Her support network of friends and family remained a crucial part of her life, providing the encouragement and strength she needed.

One evening, as they sat together on the couch, Alex took Elena's hand in his. "Thank you for giving me another chance," he said sincerely. "I know I still have a lot to prove, but I promise to keep working on being a better person and partner."

Elena looked into his eyes, seeing a mix of determination and vulnerability. "I hope you do, Alex," she replied. "I want to believe that we can make this work. But it has to be a partnership built on mutual respect and trust."

Their journey was far from over, but for the first time in a long while, Elena felt a glimmer of hope. She knew that the path ahead would be challenging, but she was ready to face it with resilience and strength. Together, they embarked on a journey of healing and growth, determined to create a future where love and respect could flourish.

Things went alright for a while. Elena and Alex made a concerted effort to accommodate each other, and their relationship began to stabilize. Alex's dedication to therapy and personal growth was evident, and Elena saw positive changes in his behavior. He was more considerate, less controlling, and genuinely interested in her well-being.

Elena, too, worked on rebuilding trust and establishing new boundaries. She continued to thrive in her job, finding fulfillment and confidence in her professional life. Her independence became a cornerstone of their renewed relationship, and Alex respected her need for space and autonomy. They communicated more openly, addressing issues before they could fester into bigger problems.

They started to enjoy their time together again, rediscovering the joy and connection that had initially brought them together. Weekend getaways, cozy nights at home, and shared hobbies helped to rekindle their bond. Alex's support extended to Elena's family, as he made genuine efforts to rebuild bridges and earn their trust.

One sunny afternoon, they took a long walk through a nearby park, enjoying the serenity and each other's company. "I'm proud of how far we've come," Alex said, squeezing Elena's hand. "I know it hasn't been easy, but I'm committed to making this work."

Elena smiled, feeling a warmth in her heart. "I am too, Alex. We've both grown a lot. I just want us to keep moving forward, together."

As the months passed, they continued to navigate their relationship with care and attention. They celebrated small victories and learned from their setbacks. Alex's business troubles persisted, but he handled them with a newfound maturity, avoiding the destructive patterns of the past. Elena stood by his side, offering support without compromising her own needs and ambitions.

Despite the improvements, there were moments of tension and doubt. Trust took time to rebuild, and both Elena and Alex had to confront their fears and insecurities. Alex occasionally slipped into old habits, and Elena had to remind him of the promises he had made. However, these instances became less frequent as they both worked to sustain the positive changes in their relationship.

One evening, while preparing dinner together, Alex paused and looked at Elena. "I want you to know that I'm grateful for your patience and understanding," he said softly. "I know I've put you through a lot, but I'm committed to being the partner you deserve."

Elena nodded, feeling a mix of gratitude and hope. "We've both worked hard to get here, Alex. Let's keep supporting each other and growing together."

Their relationship was a work in progress, marked by both challenges and triumphs. Yet, the effort they put into accommodating each other and fostering mutual respect laid the foundation for a stronger, healthier partnership. As they faced the future together, Elena remained cautiously optimistic, ready to embrace whatever came next with resilience and determination.

Chapter 5: Alex left abruptly

One crisp summer morning, just as Elena was settling into a comfortable routine, Alex abruptly announced he was leaving for a road trip with his kids. The news came out of nowhere, shaking the stability they had painstakingly built.

"I need to spend some quality time with my kids," Alex explained, his tone matter-of-fact. "It's been a while since we had an adventure together."

Elena was taken aback by the suddenness of his decision. They had discussed many things, but this trip had never come up. "When did you plan this?" she asked, trying to keep her voice steady.

"I've been thinking about it for a while," Alex replied, avoiding her gaze. "I just need to reconnect with them."

Elena nodded, though unease churned in her stomach. "Okay, I understand. When are you leaving?"

"Tomorrow," he said, confirming the abruptness of the decision. "We'll be gone for a couple of weeks."

The next morning, Alex packed his bags and loaded his kids into the car. Elena stood by, watching as they prepared to leave. She felt a mix of sadness and confusion. This trip seemed so sudden, so poorly communicated. But she knew better than to protest. "Have a great time," she said, forcing a smile. "Be safe."

Alex gave her a quick hug and a kiss on the cheek. "We will. I'll call you when I can."

As Alex and his kids drove away, Elena felt a strange emptiness settle over her. The house, usually filled with their dynamic energy, felt eerily quiet. She tried to focus on work and her daily routines, but a nagging worry lingered in the back of her mind. Why had Alex chosen now to leave so suddenly? What was really going on?

Over the next couple of weeks, Alex's calls and messages were sporadic. When he did contact her, he seemed distracted and distant. Elena tried to brush off her concerns, telling herself that he was just focusing on his kids. But the unease grew stronger with each passing day.

To cope with the uncertainty, Elena threw herself into her job. She spent long hours at the office, finding solace in her work and the support of her colleagues. She also reconnected with friends, seeking their company and advice. They listened to her worries and encouraged her to stay strong.

One evening, while chatting with a close friend over coffee, Elena voiced her fears. "Do you think I'm overreacting? It just feels like something's off."

Her friend shook her head. "Trust your instincts, Elena. If something doesn't feel right, there's probably a reason. Just be careful and take care of yourself."

Elena took those words to heart. She decided to give Alex the benefit of the doubt for now, but she remained vigilant. She would wait for him to return and see if things changed. If they didn't, she knew she had the strength and support to make the right decisions for her future.

When Alex finally returned, he was visibly different. The carefree demeanor he had left with was replaced by an air of tension and unease. Elena greeted him warmly, but her eyes searched for answers.

"How was the trip?" she asked, trying to keep the conversation light.

"It was good," Alex replied, but his smile didn't reach his eyes. "We had some good moments."

As they settled back into their routine, Elena couldn't shake the feeling that something had shifted. Alex was more withdrawn, and the open communication they had worked so hard to establish seemed to have evaporated. Elena knew she had to confront him, but she wanted to choose the right moment.

One evening, as they sat down for dinner, Elena took a deep breath. "Alex, I need to talk to you about something. I feel like you've been distant since you got back. Is there something going on?"

Alex looked at her, his eyes filled with a mix of guilt and frustration. "It's just... everything. The business, the kids, us. It's all overwhelming."

Elena reached out and took his hand. "I understand, but we need to face these things together. We can't go back to how things were before. We need to be honest with each other."

Alex nodded, but the road ahead was clearly going to be a challenging one. Elena knew that trust had to be rebuilt once more, and this time, she was determined to keep her eyes wide open.

During Alex's road trip, his birthday came and went. Elena found herself unable to bring herself to wish him. The distance between them felt wider than ever, and her unease had grown into a deep-seated concern.

On the morning of his birthday, Elena sat at the kitchen table, staring at her phone. A message to Alex sat unsent, the words "Happy Birthday" feeling hollow and forced. She knew she should send it, but something in her resisted. Her trust in him was eroded, and she couldn't shake the feeling that there was more to this trip than he had let on.

Throughout the day, she kept busy with work, trying to push her worries aside. But as evening approached, the weight of the unsent message hung heavy on her heart. She confided in a close friend, seeking solace and advice.

"I feel terrible for not wishing him a happy birthday," Elena admitted, her voice trembling. "But I just can't bring myself to do it. Something feels so wrong."

Her friend listened patiently, offering a comforting presence. "Elena, it's okay to trust your instincts. If you're not ready to reach out, don't force yourself. You've been through a lot, and it's important to prioritize your own feelings right now."

Elena nodded, grateful for the support. She knew her friend was right. She needed to take care of herself first. That night, she allowed herself to feel the full weight of her emotions, acknowledging the pain and confusion that had built up over the past weeks.

When Alex finally returned from his trip, Elena noticed a subtle tension in his demeanor. He seemed preoccupied, his thoughts elsewhere. She greeted him warmly but couldn't ignore the gnawing uncertainty that had taken root in her heart.

"How was your trip?" she asked, trying to gauge his mood.

"It was fine," Alex replied curtly. "The kids had a good time. That's all that matters."

Elena forced a smile, deciding not to mention his birthday. She felt guilty, but her unresolved feelings of distrust and betrayal kept her from reaching out. As they settled back into their routine, Elena struggled with her inner turmoil, feeling a growing disconnect between them.

One evening, as they sat together on the couch, Elena mustered the courage to address the elephant in the room. "Alex, can we talk about something?" she began, her voice steady but filled with emotion. "I didn't wish you a happy birthday while you were away. I wanted to, but I just couldn't."

Alex looked at her, his expression a mix of surprise and hurt. "Why?" he asked, his voice barely above a whisper.

Elena took a deep breath, choosing her words carefully. "Because things haven't felt right between us. You've been distant, and I've been feeling more and more uncertain about us. I didn't know how to reach out to you without feeling like I was pretending everything was okay when it wasn't."

Alex sighed, rubbing his temples. "I get it, Elena. This trip was supposed to be a way for me to clear my head, but it seems like it's caused more problems."

"We need to communicate better," Elena said, her voice firm. "We need to be honest with each other about what we're feeling. I can't go on like this, constantly doubting and worrying."

Alex nodded, his expression somber. "You're right. I haven't been fair to you. I've been struggling with a lot, and instead of sharing it with you, I pushed you away."

The conversation marked a turning point for both of them. They knew that their relationship required more than just promises and good intentions. It needed transparency, trust, and mutual respect. As they faced the challenges ahead, Elena and Alex committed to working through their issues together, knowing that the road to healing would be long and arduous.

As time went by, Elena and Alex's relationship continued to ride a rollercoaster of emotions. Moments of connection and joy were often overshadowed by periods of tension and doubt. Elena found herself constantly questioning their future, seeking clarity and commitment in a sea of uncertainty.

One crisp morning, as they sat together in their favorite café, Elena decided it was time to address the lingering issues that plagued their relationship. She took a deep breath, her resolve firm. "Alex, we need to talk about where we're headed," she began, her voice steady but filled with urgency. "I can't keep living in this state of uncertainty. I need clarity and commitment from you."

Alex looked at her, his expression a mix of surprise and defensiveness. "What do you mean, Elena? I thought we were doing better."

Elena shook her head, her frustration bubbling to the surface. "We've had our good moments, yes. But we also have constant ups and downs. I can't keep ignoring the signs that something isn't right. I need to know if you're truly committed to making this work."

Alex sighed, running a hand through his hair. "Elena, I've been trying. But it's not easy. We both have our issues to deal with."

"I understand that," Elena replied, her tone softening. "But I need more than just trying. I need to know that you're in this for the long haul. That you're willing to put in the effort to build a solid foundation for us."

For a moment, silence hung between them. Alex stared at his coffee, deep in thought. Finally, he looked up, his eyes meeting Elena's. "I am committed to us, Elena. But I also need to be honest. I have a lot of things to work through, both personally and professionally. It's going to take time."

Elena nodded, appreciating his honesty. "I understand that, Alex. But we can't keep putting our relationship on hold because of those things. We need to grow together, support each other, and build a future that we both want."

Alex reached across the table, taking her hand in his. "I want that too, Elena. I really do. Let's take this step by step, and make sure we're both on the same page."

Over the following weeks, Elena and Alex made a concerted effort to communicate more openly and honestly. They set aside time each week to discuss their feelings, their goals, and their concerns. It wasn't easy, and there were still moments of frustration and misunderstanding, but they were committed to finding a path forward together.

Elena continued to excel at her job, drawing strength and confidence from her achievements. She also made a point to nurture her friendships and maintain her independence, ensuring she had a strong support network outside of her relationship with Alex.

One evening, as they walked hand in hand through the city park, Elena felt a renewed sense of hope. "We've come a long way," she said, leaning her head on Alex's shoulder. "I know we still have a lot to work on, but I'm glad we're facing it together."

Alex smiled, squeezing her hand. "Me too, Elena. I know it's not always been easy, but I believe in us. I believe we can make this work."

As they continued their journey, Elena remained vigilant, mindful of the need for ongoing effort and commitment. She knew that the road ahead would be filled with challenges, but she was ready to face them with resilience and determination. Together, she and Alex were determined to build a future based on trust, respect, and unwavering support for each other.

As Elena pursued her new career and found fulfillment in her professional life, she couldn't help but notice that Alex's business challenges persisted. Despite their efforts to focus on their relationship and maintain boundaries, Elena often found herself drawn back into helping Alex with his business affairs.

At first, it started with simple advice or lending an ear when Alex needed to vent about work. Elena, wanting to be supportive and seeing an opportunity to contribute positively to their relationship, willingly offered her insights and assistance. She believed that by helping Alex navigate his business troubles, they could strengthen their partnership and build a stronger foundation.

However, as time went on, Elena realized that her involvement in Alex's business affairs was becoming more demanding. Late-night calls, urgent meetings, and constant stress began to encroach on their personal time together. Despite her best intentions, she felt overwhelmed and stretched thin between her own career aspirations and the demands of supporting Alex.

One evening, after a particularly stressful day at work followed by hours spent assisting Alex with a critical client issue, Elena sat quietly in their living room, feeling exhausted and conflicted. Alex noticed her subdued demeanor and sat down beside her, concern etched on his face.

"Elena, are you okay?" Alex asked softly, reaching out to gently touch her arm.

Elena sighed, running a hand through her hair. "I don't know, Alex. I want to support you, but I feel like I'm sacrificing too much of myself in the process. I have my own career goals and aspirations, and sometimes I feel like they're being overshadowed by your business challenges."

Alex nodded, his expression thoughtful. "I'm sorry, Elena. I didn't mean for it to get this overwhelming. I appreciate everything you've done for me, but I don't want it to come at the expense of your happiness and well-being."

Elena looked at him, feeling a mixture of relief and frustration. "I know you didn't mean to, Alex. But I need to find a balance. I can't keep neglecting my own needs and ambitions."

They sat in silence for a moment, each lost in their own thoughts. Finally, Alex spoke up, his voice earnest. "You're right, Elena. I need to take more responsibility for my business. I can't rely on you to solve every problem for me. I want us to support each other equally, in both our personal and professional lives."

Elena nodded, grateful for his understanding. "I want that too, Alex. Let's work together to find a better balance. I believe we can support each other without losing sight of our individual goals."

From that day forward, Elena and Alex made a conscious effort to redefine their roles in each other's lives. Alex took steps to manage his business more independently, seeking professional advice and developing a stronger network of support. Elena, in turn, prioritized her own career development while offering Alex moral support and encouragement from a healthy distance.

They continued to face challenges and occasional setbacks, but their commitment to mutual respect, clear communication, and personal growth strengthened their bond. Elena learned to set boundaries and prioritize self-care, while Alex embraced his responsibilities with newfound determination and resilience.

Together, they navigated the complexities of their intertwined lives, learning valuable lessons about partnership, independence, and the importance of supporting each other's individual journeys. As they faced the future, Elena and Alex were determined to build a relationship based on equality, understanding, and shared aspirations for a fulfilling life together.

In September, as Elena's birthday approached, both she and Alex found themselves swept up in their respective business obligations. Elena had a crucial business trip scheduled, requiring her to be away during her birthday. Meanwhile, Alex also had travel commitments that coincided with the same period.

Elena's trip took her to a bustling city where she attended meetings, networked with industry leaders, and worked tirelessly to advance her career goals. Despite the professional focus, she couldn't help but feel a twinge of disappointment about being away from Alex and missing out on celebrating her birthday with him.

On the morning of her birthday, Elena woke up in a hotel room far from home. She checked her phone, finding heartfelt messages and well-wishes from friends and family. There was also a message from Alex, sent in the early hours before he boarded his flight.

"Happy Birthday, Elena," the message read. "I wish I could be there with you today. I hope your day is filled with everything you deserve. I love you."

Elena smiled, touched by Alex's words. Despite the distance and their busy schedules, his gesture reminded her of the bond they shared. She replied with a heartfelt thank you, expressing her understanding of their current circumstances and looking forward to celebrating together when they were both back home.

Throughout the day, Elena immersed herself in her work, finding fulfillment in her accomplishments and the knowledge that she was making strides in her career. Colleagues took her out for a birthday lunch, and she received thoughtful gifts from clients she had built strong relationships with over the years.

Meanwhile, Alex's travels kept him occupied with meetings and site visits. He thought of Elena often, wishing he could be by her side to celebrate this special day. During a brief break, he called her, their conversation filled with laughter and fond reminiscences of past birthdays they had celebrated together.

That evening, despite the distance, they found a way to connect virtually. Alex surprised Elena with a video call, where he had arranged for a small cake to be delivered to her hotel room. They sang happy birthday together, laughing at the makeshift celebration.

"I wish I could give you a proper celebration," Alex said sincerely, his eyes reflecting his regret.

Elena shook her head, her heart full. "This is perfect, Alex. Thank you for making my birthday special, even from afar."

As they talked late into the night, sharing stories and dreams for the future, Elena felt a renewed sense of gratitude for Alex and their relationship. Despite the challenges and the miles between them, their love and commitment remained steadfast. They vowed to make up for the missed celebration once they were reunited, cherishing every moment they could spend together.

Elena: "Hey, Alex! How's your trip going? It must be amazing to be in Europe."

Alex: *hesitates* "Oh, it's been good. Really busy with meetings and all."

Elena: "That's great to hear! Any chance you get to do some sightseeing?"

Alex: *pauses, feeling uneasy* "Yeah, a bit here and there. You know how these trips go, though. Mostly work."

Elena: *sensing something* "Is everything okay, Alex? You sound a bit off."

Alex: *takes a deep breath* "Actually, there's something I need to tell you, Elena. I... I haven't been entirely honest."

Elena: *worriedly* "What do you mean? What's going on?"

Alex: *explains reluctantly* "I didn't want to worry you, but... the truth is, I'm not in Europe for work. I'm actually here because... I needed some time to think."

Elena: *confused and concerned* "Time to think? About what?"

Alex: *sighs* "About us. About where we're headed. I've been feeling overwhelmed with everything lately, and I needed some space to sort things out."

Elena: *quietly* "I see... I wish you had told me sooner, Alex."

Alex: *apologetically* "I know, and I'm sorry for keeping this from you. It wasn't fair. But please believe me, Elena, it's not about us. It's about me figuring things out."

Elena: *takes a moment to process* "Okay... I appreciate you being honest now. Just... please keep me in the loop, Alex. We're in this together, remember?"

Alex: *softly* "I will, Elena. I promise."

Elena: *with resolve* "Alright. Take your time, but don't shut me out, okay?"

Alex: *gratefully* "I won't. Thank you for understanding, Elena. I love you."

Elena: *affectionately* "I love you too, Alex. We'll figure this out, together."

In the weeks that followed, Elena returned home, and Alex's travels also came to an end. They made time for each other, relishing in the simple joys of being together. Elena's birthday celebration became a cherished memory, a testament to their ability to support and uplift each other, no matter the distance or obstacles they faced.

Elena and Alex spent a delightful afternoon browsing through jewelry stores, their hearts set on finding the perfect ring to symbolize their commitment to each other. With each shop they visited, excitement grew as they envisioned their future together. They carefully examined various designs, discussing what aspects appealed to each of them. Alex, known for his meticulous nature, compared different metals and gemstones, while Elena, with her eye for elegance, focused on intricate details and settings.

Between visits to jewelers, they paused at a cozy café, sipping on lattes and playfully sketching ideas for their wedding. Elena dreamed of an outdoor ceremony surrounded by nature's beauty, while Alex, always the pragmatist, made notes about logistics and guest lists. Together, they brainstormed ways to blend their cultural traditions into the celebration, eager to create an event that would reflect their unique personalities and shared values.

As the day wound down, they strolled hand in hand through a park, reflecting on their journey together and the excitement of planning their future. For Elena and Alex, this day of shopping for rings and making wedding plans wasn't just about the material aspects; it was a joyful affirmation of their love and commitment to building a life together.

Elena: "Hey, Alex... I can tell something's not right. You're not telling me everything, are you?"

Alex: *hesitates, caught off guard* "Um... what do you mean?"

Elena: *gently but firmly* "Alex, I know you well enough to sense when something's bothering you. Please, just be honest with me."

Alex: *sighs, realizing he's been caught* "Okay, you're right. I haven't been entirely truthful."

Elena: *concerned* "What's going on, Alex? Please tell me."

Alex: *pauses, choosing his words carefully* "I didn't want to worry you, but... the truth is, I'm not in Europe for work. I... I needed some time alone."

Elena: *taken aback* "Alone? Why didn't you tell me this before?"

Alex: *hesitantly* "I thought... I thought I could sort things out on my own. I didn't want to burden you."

Elena: *softly* "Alex, you're not a burden. We're supposed to share these things with each other."

Alex: *regretfully* "I know, and I'm sorry for not being honest sooner."

Elena: *emotionally* "I just want to understand, Alex. What's going on that you couldn't talk to me about?"

Alex: *opens up* "I've been feeling overwhelmed with everything... with work, with us... I needed some space to think things through."

Elena: *nods, trying to be supportive* "I understand, but please don't shut me out, Alex. We're a team, remember?"

Alex: *softly* "I know, Elena. I'm sorry. I should've trusted you with this."

Elena: *reassuringly* "It's okay. Just... promise me you'll keep me in the loop from now on."

Alex: *nodding earnestly* "I promise, Elena. I won't shut you out again."

Elena: *reaches out emotionally* "I love you, Alex. We'll figure this out together."

Alex: *relieved* "I love you too, Elena. Thank you for understanding."

Met up with the person that Elena didn't want him to

Elena: "Alex, I have to ask you something. Are you being completely honest with me?"

Alex: *pauses, caught off guard* "What do you mean?"

Elena: *calmly but with concern* "I've been feeling like something's off lately. Are you sure there's nothing you need to tell me?"

Alex: *hesitates, trying to find the right words* "Elena, I... I haven't been entirely truthful."

Elena: *heart sinking* "What do you mean, Alex? Please, just tell me."

Alex: *sighs heavily* "I... I met up with my ex while I was in Europe. We've been talking, secretly."

Elena: *shocked and hurt* "Your ex? Alex, why didn't you tell me this before?"

Alex: *regretfully* "I didn't know how to... I didn't want to hurt you."

Elena: *tears welling up* "But keeping it from me hurts even more, Alex. How could you?"

Alex: *desperately* "I'm so sorry, Elena. It wasn't planned... It just happened, and I didn't know how to handle it."

Elena: *struggling to stay composed* "I trusted you, Alex. I thought we were building a future together."

Alex: *pleadingly* "Elena, please believe me, it's not about us. I've been confused, and I needed time to sort out my feelings."

Elena: *voice trembling* "Do you still... love me?"

Alex: *quickly* "Yes, Elena, I do. It's just... I don't know what I want right now."

Elena: *broken-hearted* "I need time to think too, Alex. I can't... I can't do this right now."

Alex: *desperately reaching out* "Please, Elena, don't shut me out. I want to fix this."

Elena: *with finality* "I need some space, Alex. I need to figure out if I can trust you again."

Alex: *softly* "I understand. I'm so sorry, Elena."

Elena: *hangs up, overwhelmed with emotions*

Elena: "Alex, I can't ignore this anymore. I know you've been lying to me about your ex."

Alex: *defensively* "What are you talking about, Elena? I've told you everything."

Elena: "I found the messages, Alex. You've been corresponding with her behind my back."

Alex: *hesitates, trying to maintain his facade* "Elena, it's not what you think. We were just catching up, that's all."

Elena: *upset* "Catching up? How could you keep this from me?"

Alex: *frustrated* "It's not a big deal, Elena. It's just old friends talking."

Elena: *tearfully* "You lied to me, Alex. How can I trust you now?"

Alex: *trying to placate her* "Elena, please, don't overreact. It doesn't mean anything."

Elena: *emotionally* "But it means everything to me, Alex. I thought we were building a future together."

Alex: *growing defensive* "You're blowing this out of proportion. It's just harmless conversation."

Elena: *shaken* "I can't believe you're making excuses. You've been gaslighting me, Alex."

Alex: *denying vehemently* "I'm not gaslighting you! You're being paranoid."

Elena: *firmly* "I deserve better than this, Alex. I need some time to think."

Alex: *desperately* "Please, Elena, don't leave. I'll stop talking to her, I promise."

Elena: *with resolve* "I need space, Alex. I need to figure out if I can trust you again."

Alex: *silently, realizing the consequences of his actions*

Elena sat alone in the dim light of her living room, the weight of betrayal pressing heavily on her chest. Her heart ached, and her thoughts raced in a chaotic loop as she tried to make sense of everything. The messages she had found between Alex and his ex replayed in her mind, each one a dagger that pierced her trust.

She had always prided herself on her intuition, but now she questioned everything. How could she have missed the signs? How had she been so blind to Alex's deceit? The pain of his betrayal was compounded by the self-doubt it had sown within her.

Elena's emotions swung wildly from anger to sadness, and she struggled to find clarity amidst the storm. She replayed their conversations over and over, remembering every lie, every dismissive comment, and every time Alex had made her feel like she was the problem. The realization that he had been gaslighting her was like a slap in the face.

She tried to focus on the facts. Alex had lied to her repeatedly. He had maintained a secret correspondence with his ex, and when confronted, he had dismissed her feelings and invalidated her concerns. The betrayal was not just in his actions but in his blatant disregard for her emotional well-being.

Elena sought solace in writing, pouring her heart into her journal. She detailed every interaction, every feeling, and every doubt. The act of writing helped her to process her emotions and gain a clearer perspective. She wrote about the future she had envisioned with Alex and how it now seemed like a mirage, a beautiful illusion shattered by his lies.

She reached out to her closest friends, seeking their support and advice. Their reactions varied from shock to anger on her behalf, but they all had one thing in common: they reminded her of her worth and the importance of self-respect. They urged her to prioritize her own well-being and not to let Alex's betrayal define her.

Elena also took long walks to clear her mind, finding some peace in the rhythm of her footsteps and the beauty of nature. She would often sit by a quiet pond, watching the ripples on the water's surface, and contemplate her next steps. The process of healing was slow and painful, but each day brought a tiny bit more clarity.

In her moments of introspection, Elena recognized that dealing with betrayal was not just about understanding Alex's actions but also about rediscovering herself. She needed to rebuild her confidence, trust her instincts again, and find a way to move forward without the shadow of doubt hanging over her.

The path ahead was uncertain, and the wound in her heart was deep, but Elena resolved to take it one day at a time. She knew that healing was a journey, and while Alex's betrayal had marked the end of one chapter, it also signaled the beginning of another—one where she would emerge stronger, wiser, and more resilient.

Elena decided to put on a brave face and pretend that everything was normal, convincing herself that she could work things out with Alex. She smiled through her pain, hoping that if she acted as if everything was fine, the cracks in their relationship would somehow mend themselves.

Mornings were the hardest. She would wake up with a knot in her stomach, the first thoughts in her mind always about Alex and his betrayal. But she would force herself to get up, get dressed, and go about her day. She would prepare breakfast, making his favorite coffee just the way he liked it, and greet him with a smile as if nothing had changed.

At work, she maintained her usual professionalism, even though her mind often wandered back to the messages she had found. She would catch herself staring blankly at her computer screen, the weight of her emotions pressing down on her, but she would shake it off and refocus. Her colleagues noticed that she seemed quieter than usual, but she brushed off their concerns with a practiced laugh and a reassuring comment about being busy.

In the evenings, she and Alex would sit down for dinner together. She would ask about his day, listen to his stories, and laugh at his jokes, all the while feeling a growing sense of disconnection. When he looked at her with those same eyes that had once made her feel so loved, she couldn't help but wonder how he could lie so easily. She longed to confront him again, to demand the truth, but the fear of his dismissive responses held her back.

Deep inside, the turmoil raged on. Elena struggled with her conflicting emotions—love for the man she had planned to spend her life with, and anger and hurt from his betrayal. She would lie awake at night, staring at the ceiling, her mind racing with unanswered questions and doubts. She felt trapped between her desire to make things work and the painful reality of Alex's actions.

Elena found herself constantly analyzing every word, every action. Was he truly sorry, or was he just saying what he thought she wanted to hear? Could she ever trust him again, or was she just fooling herself? These thoughts consumed her, leaving her feeling exhausted and emotionally drained.

She sought solace in small moments of solitude. When Alex was out or busy, she would retreat to her favorite reading nook, a cozy corner filled with books and soft pillows. She would lose herself in stories, finding temporary escape from her own reality. Sometimes, she would write in her journal, pouring out her frustrations and fears, the pages becoming a silent witness to her inner turmoil.

Despite her efforts to act like everything was normal, the strain began to show. She became more irritable, her patience wearing thin. Little things that she used to overlook now felt like insurmountable obstacles. The pressure of maintaining the facade was taking its toll, and she felt herself slipping.

Friends and family, sensing something was wrong, would ask if she was okay. Elena would smile and assure them that everything was fine, but inside, she felt like she was crumbling. The weight of the deception, both Alex's and her own, was becoming too much to bear.

Elena knew she couldn't keep up the act forever. The cracks were starting to show, and pretending was no longer enough to hold things together. She realized that she needed to confront her feelings and face the reality of the situation. It was a painful and daunting prospect, but she knew that in order to find true peace and healing, she had to stop pretending and start being honest with herself—and with Alex.

Elena felt completely lost. Her once bright and hopeful future now seemed shrouded in uncertainty and pain. With each passing day, the weight of Alex's betrayal grew heavier, and she found herself struggling to find a way forward. Her heart ached with the realization that the man she had loved and trusted was more concerned with his own ego than with the damage he had caused.

Alex, with his inflated sense of self-importance, was always right and never wrong in his own eyes. His office was filled with people who catered to his every whim, their livelihoods dependent on keeping him happy. They flattered him, boosted his ego, and validated his every decision, no matter how misguided. In this environment, Alex thrived, oblivious to the pain he was causing Elena.

Elena tried to reach out to Alex, to explain how deeply hurt she was by his actions. She hoped that, somehow, he would understand and show some remorse. But every attempt was met with the same dismissive arrogance.

Elena: "Alex, I need to talk to you about how I'm feeling. This whole situation with your ex has really hurt me."

Alex: *impatiently* "Elena, you're overreacting again. We've been over this. There's nothing to talk about."

Elena: *frustrated* "But it matters to me! I need to know that you care about my feelings."

Alex: *coldly* "I care about you, but I can't keep catering to your insecurities. You need to get over it."

Feeling the sting of his words, Elena realized that getting through to Alex was impossible. His ego, constantly fueled by his office sycophants, left no room for self-reflection or empathy. He was surrounded by people who only told him what he wanted to hear, reinforcing his belief that he was always right.

In her moments of solitude, Elena found herself spiraling into a deep sense of isolation. She had no one to turn to—her friends and family were either distant or unaware of the full extent of her pain. The one person she had always counted on for support and understanding was the very source of her anguish.

One evening, feeling utterly alone, Elena decided to take a walk to clear her mind. The cool night air provided some comfort as she wandered aimlessly through the quiet streets. She found herself at a small park, where she sat on a bench and let her thoughts flow.

Elena's thoughts: "How did it come to this? How did I end up feeling so trapped and alone? I thought Alex loved me, but all he seems to care about is himself. I can't keep pretending that everything is fine. I need to find a way out of this darkness."

Tears streamed down her face as she realized that the life she had envisioned with Alex was no longer possible. She felt an overwhelming sense of loss, not just for the relationship, but for the dreams and plans that had crumbled before her eyes.

As the days turned into weeks, Elena continued to struggle with her emotions. She put on a brave face for the world, but inside, she was falling apart. The constant pressure to act like everything was normal, coupled with Alex's dismissive attitude, was slowly eroding her sense of self-worth.

In a moment of clarity, Elena realized that she needed to take control of her own destiny. She couldn't rely on Alex or anyone else to validate her feelings or give her the strength to move forward. She had to find it within herself.

Determined to reclaim her life, Elena began to seek out small moments of joy and self-care. She started journaling more regularly, finding solace in expressing her thoughts and emotions on paper. She reconnected with hobbies that had once brought her happiness, such as painting and reading. These activities provided a much-needed escape and allowed her to rediscover parts of herself that had been overshadowed by her relationship with Alex.

Elena also started attending a local support group for people dealing with emotional trauma. Though it was difficult to open up at first, she found comfort in the shared experiences and support of others who had faced similar challenges. Slowly, she began to rebuild her confidence and sense of self-worth.

Through this journey, Elena realized that healing was not a linear process. There were days when the pain seemed insurmountable, but there were also moments of light and hope. She learned to be patient with herself and to acknowledge her progress, no matter how small.

As Elena grew stronger, she started to distance herself emotionally from Alex. She recognized that she deserved better than to be with someone who disregarded her feelings and fueled his own ego at her expense. It was a difficult and painful decision, but she knew that letting go of Alex was the only way to truly heal and move forward.

In the end, Elena emerged from the darkness with a newfound sense of strength and resilience. She had faced betrayal and heartache, but she had also discovered her own inner power. With time, she knew she would continue to heal and create a life filled with genuine love, respect, and happiness.

As Elena grappled with her own emotions and the betrayal she felt, she couldn't help but notice how Alex's narcissistic behavior extended beyond their relationship and into his role as a father. His interactions with his children, Emma and Jake, were just another part of the carefully crafted facade he maintained. To outsiders, Alex appeared to be the perfect father, always involved in his children's lives and providing for their every need. But Elena saw through the illusion.

She noticed how Alex kept Emma and Jake dependent on him, ensuring that they relied on his approval and guidance for everything. He made decisions for them, big and small, stifling their independence and self-confidence.

Emma: "Dad, I just don't know what to do with my life. I can't decide on a career or find a job that interests me. I feel like I'm wasting my time. I want to travel, go to concerts, maybe even find a relationship abroad."

Alex: *smiling but with a controlling undertone* "Emma, you don't need to worry about that. Just stay here and live on unemployment insurance plus I can always help you with whatever you need. There's no rush to find a job right now, and travelling don't have to wait. I can buy you tickets and sponsor all your friends too."

Emma: "Dad, can I go to the Nashville with my friends this weekend? Are you going to fund our trip?"

Alex: *"Absolutely, as much as you want.* I would do anything for you."

Elena saw how Alex's control extended to their hobbies, friendships, and even their future plans. Emma often looked to their father for approval, second-guessing their own desires and instincts. Alex's subtle manipulation ensured they stayed within the boundaries he set, under the guise of being a protective and involved parent.

At family gatherings, Alex's facade was on full display. He would boast about his children's accomplishments, taking credit for their successes while subtly downplaying their independent efforts.

Alex: "Emma did great on her science project, didn't she? I spent hours helping her research and build the model."

Alex: "Jake's piano recital was wonderful. We practiced together every evening."

Elena felt a pang of sadness each time she witnessed these interactions. She saw the confusion and frustration in Emma and Jake's eyes, as they struggled to navigate their father's expectations and their own burgeoning sense of self. They loved their father, but his constant need for control left them feeling suffocated and unsure of their own capabilities.

In her private moments, Elena reflected on how Alex's behavior had affected their children. She worried about the long-term impact of his manipulative parenting style. She knew that Emma and Jake needed to learn to trust their own judgments, make their own mistakes, and grow into independent, confident individuals.

One evening, after another stifling family dinner where Alex dominated the conversation and decisions, Elena decided to talk to

Emma and Jake. She wanted to offer them the support and encouragement they deserved.

Elena: "Emma, Jake, can we talk for a minute?"

Emma: *curiously* "Sure, Mom. What's up?"

Jake: *nervously* "Is something wrong?"

Elena: *softly* "I just want you both to know that it's okay to have your own opinions and make your own choices. You don't always have to rely on your dad or me for everything. You're both smart and capable."

Emma: *hesitantly* "But Dad always says he knows what's best for us."

Elena: *gently* "I know he means well, but it's important for you to learn to trust yourselves too. It's okay to explore your interests and make decisions, even if they're different from what your dad suggests."

Jake: *thoughtfully* "You mean we can do things on our own?"

Elena: *encouragingly* "Yes, Jake. You can. While your dad can be here to support you, no matter what, it is important that you are independent."

As the weeks passed, Elena continued to offer her own 2 children the space to grow and make their own choices. She encouraged Emma to join the soccer team and supported Jake's desire to spend time with his friends. Slowly, she saw them begin to trust their own instincts and develop a sense of independence.

Elena's journey was far from over, but she found strength in knowing that she was helping her children break free from Alex's controlling influence. She hoped that, in time, they would learn to navigate the complexities of their father's narcissism and build lives filled with confidence and self-assurance.

Elena sat in her favorite chair, staring out the window at the rain tapping softly against the glass. She felt a profound sense of disbelief and sorrow as she thought about how deeply intertwined her life had become with Alex's. The man she once believed to be her soulmate had revealed himself to be a psychological monster, leaving her feeling trapped and betrayed.

How had she not seen it? How had she allowed herself to be drawn into his web so completely?

The realization of Alex's true nature came to her in waves. At first, it was just a nagging doubt, a small voice in the back of her mind questioning his behavior. But as the evidence mounted—the messages with his ex, his dismissive responses, his manipulative control over their children—that doubt grew into a devastating truth.

Elena's thoughts: "I thought he was my everything. How did I get so entangled with someone I didn't truly know? How did I miss all the signs?"

Reflecting on their relationship, Elena saw how Alex's charm had blinded her to the red flags. He had been so attentive, so loving in the beginning. His grand gestures and constant attention had made her feel special, cherished. It was easy to overlook the subtle ways he began to control her life, framing it as care and concern.

Early Signs of Control:

- **Subtle Isolation:** Alex would often suggest that they spend time together instead of with her friends or family. He would say things like, "Why don't we have a quiet night in? I just want to be with you," making her feel guilty for wanting to see others.
- **Erosion of Self-Esteem:** His seemingly harmless jokes about her choices and appearance gradually eroded her confidence. "Are you sure you want to wear that? It's not really your color," he would say, always with a smile that made her doubt her own judgment.
- **Micromanaging Decisions:** From what she wore to how she spent her free time, Alex's opinion always seemed to carry more weight. "Let me handle it, I know what's best," was a

common refrain.

As these patterns emerged, Elena realized how Alex had systematically undermined her independence. He had created an environment where she felt constantly dependent on his approval and guidance. And when their children came along, he extended this control to them, ensuring they too relied on him.

The facade Alex presented to the outside world only deepened Elena's isolation. He was charming and charismatic, a model partner and father in the eyes of friends and colleagues. People often remarked on how lucky she was to have him, and she had believed it herself for so long.

Friends and Colleagues' Perception:

- **Colleagues:** "Alex is such a great guy. He always talks about how much he loves you and the kids."
- **Friends:** "You and Alex seem like the perfect couple. He's so attentive and caring."

These comments, meant to be complimentary, only made Elena feel more trapped. How could she tell anyone what was really happening when everyone saw him as the perfect man?

As the realization of Alex's true nature settled in, Elena felt a mix of anger, betrayal, and profound sadness. She had built her life around this man, trusting him implicitly, only to discover that he had manipulated and controlled her every step of the way.

Elena's Emotional Turmoil:

- **Anger:** "How could he do this to me? To us? He's been lying and manipulating us all along."
- **Betrayal:** "I gave him everything, trusted him completely, and this is how he repays me?"

- **Sadness:** "I thought we had a future together, but it was all built on lies."

Elena knew she needed to find a way out, not just for herself, but for her children. They deserved a life free from Alex's manipulative control, a chance to grow into independent and confident individuals. But the path ahead seemed daunting.

Taking the first steps towards reclaiming her life, Elena started by seeking therapy. She needed a safe space to process her emotions and gain clarity on her next steps. Through therapy, she began to understand the dynamics of narcissistic abuse and how Alex had manipulated her.

Therapist: "It's important to remember that none of this is your fault, Elena. Narcissists are very skilled at hiding their true nature and making their victims doubt themselves."

Elena also reached out to a support group for individuals who had experienced similar relationships. Hearing others' stories and sharing her own helped her feel less alone. She started to rebuild her self-esteem, learning to trust her instincts again.

Support Group Member: "I know how hard it is to break free from someone like that. But you're stronger than you think, and you deserve to be happy."

Elena began making plans to secure her and her children's future. She discreetly consulted a lawyer to understand her rights and the steps she needed to take to protect herself and her kids. She started to save money and look for a place where they could live independently from Alex.

Lawyer: "We'll ensure you and your children are protected. You have more options than you realize."

Through this painful journey, Elena discovered a resilience she didn't know she had. Each step away from Alex, each moment of self-assertion, brought her closer to the life she wanted for herself and her children. She knew it would take time and that there would be challenges ahead, but she was determined to reclaim her life and build a future where she and her children could thrive without the shadow of Alex's control.

Elena and Alex decided to see a psychologist in an attempt to salvage their relationship. Despite the deep wounds and the pervasive mistrust, Elena still hoped that professional help might bring some clarity and resolution. Alex, on the other hand, saw it as an opportunity to prove that he was right and that any issues were due to Elena's insecurities.

Their first session was tense. The psychologist, Dr. Bennett, was a calm and empathetic woman who immediately sensed the underlying tension between them. She began by asking them to share their perspectives on why they were there.

Dr. Bennett: "Thank you both for coming. I understand this isn't easy. Let's start with why you feel you need to be here. Elena, would you like to begin?"

Elena took a deep breath, feeling the weight of her emotions pressing down on her.

Elena: "I feel like we're falling apart. Alex's betrayal and the way he dismisses my feelings have made it hard for me to trust him. I want to understand if we can rebuild what we've lost."

Dr. Bennett nodded and turned to Alex.

Dr. Bennett: "And Alex, what's your perspective?"

Alex leaned back in his chair, his expression one of confident detachment.

Alex: "I think Elena is overreacting. I admit I made some mistakes, but I feel she's blowing things out of proportion. I'm here to support her and show her that we can move past this."

Dr. Bennett observed their body language and noted the stark contrast in their approaches. She decided to dig deeper.

Dr. Bennett: "Elena, can you share more about what specific actions or behaviors have hurt you?"

Elena hesitated but then spoke up, her voice trembling with emotion.

Elena: "Alex has been talking to his ex behind my back. When I confronted him, he dismissed my feelings, making me feel like I'm the one who's wrong. He controls so much of our lives, and I feel like I'm losing myself."

Dr. Bennett turned to Alex.

Dr. Bennett: "Alex, how do you respond to Elena's feelings about your behavior?"

Alex sighed, clearly irritated.

Alex: "I didn't think talking to my ex was a big deal. Elena's insecurities are the real problem here. I just want to move past this and not dwell on it."

Dr. Bennett saw the challenge ahead. Alex's narcissistic tendencies were evident, and his lack of empathy was a significant barrier.

Dr. Bennett: "Alex, it's important to understand that Elena's feelings are valid, whether or not you agree with them. Can you acknowledge how your actions might have hurt her?"

Alex's response was guarded, but he nodded reluctantly.

Alex: "I suppose I can see how she might feel that way, but I still think she's overreacting."

Dr. Bennett decided to focus on communication and empathy, hoping to break through Alex's defenses.

Dr. Bennett: "Let's work on active listening and expressing empathy. Alex, I want you to repeat back what Elena said and then share how you think she feels."

Alex looked uncomfortable but complied.

Alex: "Elena feels hurt and betrayed because I talked to my ex and dismissed her feelings. She feels like I'm controlling and she's losing herself."

Dr. Bennett nodded encouragingly.

Dr. Bennett: "Now, tell Elena how you think she feels."

Alex paused, struggling to find the right words.

Alex: "I think you feel... angry and sad. Like you're not being heard or respected."

Elena's eyes filled with tears, both from the pain of the situation and the relief of finally hearing some acknowledgment, however small, from Alex.

Dr. Bennett: "Elena, how does it feel to hear Alex express your feelings back to you?"

Elena: "It feels... better, but I need more than words. I need actions that show he understands and respects my feelings."

Dr. Bennett saw this as a critical moment to address deeper issues.

Dr. Bennett: "Alex, rebuilding trust requires consistent, genuine effort. It's not just about saying the right things but doing the right things. Are you willing to commit to this process?"

Alex hesitated, but seeing the genuine hurt in Elena's eyes, he nodded.

Alex: "Yes, I'm willing to try."

The sessions continued, with Dr. Bennett guiding them through exercises to rebuild communication and trust. They worked on setting boundaries, with Elena asserting her needs and Alex learning to respect them. There were setbacks, especially given Alex's narcissistic tendencies, but small progress was made.

Session Progress:

1. **Setting Boundaries:** Dr. Bennett helped Elena establish clear boundaries regarding Alex's communication with his ex and other behaviors that made her uncomfortable.

Dr. Bennett: "Elena, what boundaries do you need to feel safe in this relationship?"

Elena: "I need transparency. No more secret communications. And I need my feelings to be taken seriously."

1. **Building Trust:** They worked on rebuilding trust through consistent, respectful actions. Alex had to demonstrate through his behavior that he valued Elena's feelings.

Dr. Bennett: "Alex, trust is rebuilt through actions. How will you show Elena that you respect her boundaries?"

Alex: "I'll be open about my communications and check in with her about her feelings."

1. **Empathy Exercises:** Dr. Bennett introduced empathy exercises, where each would share a feeling and the other had to listen and validate it without judgment.

Dr. Bennett: "Let's practice empathy. Elena, share a recent moment that upset you."

Elena: "Last week, when you dismissed my concerns about your late meetings, it hurt."

Alex: *listening* "I see how that would hurt. I'm sorry for not considering your feelings."

Despite the small steps forward, Elena knew that the journey ahead was long and uncertain. Alex's narcissistic traits made genuine change difficult, and she had to decide if she could continue in a relationship where she might never fully feel heard or respected.

Despite the sessions with Dr. Bennett, Alex showed no genuine remorse. He continued to believe he was right, resenting Elena for the changes she was making in her life, particularly her decision to start working at a new company. His resentment and lack of empathy only deepened the chasm between them.

Elena's new job was a significant step toward reclaiming her independence. She felt a sense of accomplishment and self-worth that had been eroded during her years with Alex. However, this newfound strength was met with resistance from Alex.

Alex: *coldly* "I don't understand why you needed to take that job. We were doing fine with me providing for us. It's like you don't trust me to take care of our family."

Elena: *calmly* "I needed this job for myself, Alex. It's important for me to have my own career and independence."

Alex's resentment was palpable. He often made snide remarks about her work, belittling her accomplishments and questioning her commitment to their family.

Alex: *sarcastically* "Oh, you had a great day at work? Must be nice to be away from your responsibilities here."

Elena felt the weight of his disapproval but tried to maintain her composure. She had come to realize that his resentment was another form of control, a way to undermine her confidence and keep her dependent on him. Despite the ongoing therapy sessions, Alex's narcissistic tendencies remained unchanged.

Dr. Bennett: "Alex, it's crucial to support Elena's growth and independence. Your resentment is damaging your relationship."

Alex: *defensively* "I'm just saying what I feel. She's putting her job above our family."

Elena felt a mix of frustration and sadness. She had hoped that therapy would help Alex see the need for change, but his deep-seated narcissism and inability to empathize made genuine progress nearly impossible.

Outside of the therapy sessions, Alex's behavior grew more controlling. He would question Elena about her day in a manner that felt less like interest and more like interrogation.

Alex: "Who did you talk to at work today? Any new male colleagues?"
Elena: "Alex, I talk to lots of people at work. It's part of my job."
Alex: "I just want to know who you're spending your time with."

Elena realized that she needed to make a decision for her own well-being and that of her children. She couldn't continue to live under the oppressive weight of Alex's control and resentment. She needed to find a way to break free.

Realizing she could no longer bear the weight of her struggles alone, Elena took a brave step. She reached out to her friends and family, vulnerably sharing her pain and fears. To her surprise, she discovered a circle of love and support that she hadn't fully acknowledged before. This network, composed of people who genuinely cared for her, became her lifeline. They listened, comforted, and stood by her side, offering the strength and encouragement she desperately needed. In their embrace, Elena found a glimmer of hope and the courage to face the challenges ahead.

Elena knew she had to protect herself and her children, so she discreetly sought legal counsel. Consulting a lawyer, she gained a clear understanding of her options and the necessary steps to prepare for a possible separation from Alex. This was not just a pragmatic move; it was a significant step towards reclaiming her life. Armed with knowledge and a newfound sense of security, Elena felt empowered. She realized that she had the right to make informed decisions about her future, ensuring the safety and well-being of her family.

Therapy became a sanctuary for Elena, a place where she could rebuild her emotional resilience. Through consistent sessions, she started to see her own worth and understood the importance of a life free from Alex's toxic influence. Her therapist guided her in setting boundaries, prioritizing her well-being, and embarking on a path of healing and self-discovery. Each session was a step towards reclaiming her life, learning to love herself, and embracing the journey ahead with newfound strength. Elena's resolve was no longer just a flicker of hope; it was a blazing light guiding her towards a brighter, healthier future.

In her quest for self-discovery, Elena found solace in the pages of books. She immersed herself in stories of resilience, personal growth, and transformation, drawing parallels to her own life. These literary journeys provided her with new perspectives and insights, helping her to understand her own emotions and experiences. Through reading, Elena connected with characters who faced and overcame adversity, inspiring her to continue her own journey with renewed determination. Each book became a stepping stone, guiding her closer to her true self and reinforcing her belief in her ability to overcome her challenges. In the quiet moments spent with a book in hand, Elena found a deep sense of peace and a powerful reminder that she was not alone in her struggles.

One evening, after another tense argument about her job, Elena made a decision.

Elena: "Alex, I can't do this anymore. I need to live a life where I'm respected and valued. I'm moving out, and I'm taking the kids with me."

Alex's reaction was a mixture of disbelief and anger.

Alex: "You can't just leave. You're overreacting. We can fix this."

Elena: *firmly* "No, Alex. I've tried to make this work, but I can't continue in a relationship where I'm constantly belittled and controlled. This is for my well-being and for my children's future."

The next few weeks were challenging as Elena navigated the logistics of moving out and starting a new chapter in her life. But with each step, she felt a growing sense of liberation. Her new job provided her with financial independence, and the support from friends, family, and her therapist gave her the strength to keep moving forward.

Chapter 6: It was Christmas

Elena and Alex each spent Christmas with their respective families. Elena's Christmas was filled with the warm, familiar traditions of her childhood. She gathered with her parents and siblings around a beautifully decorated tree, sharing laughter and memories as they exchanged thoughtful gifts. The house was filled with the comforting aromas of home-cooked meals, and the day was marked by joyful conversations, festive music, and the twinkling of holiday lights. Elena cherished these moments with her family, savoring the closeness and love that surrounded her.

On the other hand, Alex celebrated Christmas with his family in a similar vein. His parents, siblings, and extended family came together, filling the house with merriment. They followed their own unique traditions, playing games, singing carols, and enjoying a sumptuous feast. The children ran around excitedly, and the adults caught up on each other's lives, creating an atmosphere of warmth and togetherness that Alex deeply appreciated.

Both Elena and Alex had planned to host a Christmas gathering with all their children together shortly after their individual family celebrations. They envisioned a joyous occasion where their blended family would come together, strengthening bonds and creating new traditions. However, as the day approached, Elena found herself struggling with an overwhelming sense of pain and sadness. The weight of her emotions became unbearable.

On the morning of their planned celebration, Elena tried her best to put on a brave face. The house was decorated festively, and the children were excitedly awaiting the arrival of their blended family. But as the hours passed, Elena's internal turmoil grew more intense. She could feel the walls closing in, her heart heavy with unspoken grief.

During a moment of quiet amidst the preparations, Elena felt a surge of panic. She couldn't bear the thought of facing everyone and pretending to be joyful when she felt anything but. Tears welled up in her eyes, and despite Alex's attempts to comfort her, the pain was too much to contain.

Without warning, Elena stormed out of the house, leaving Alex and the children in stunned silence. She needed space to breathe, to escape the suffocating weight of her emotions. Alex, understanding the depth of her distress, didn't try to stop her. Instead, he reassured the children, explaining that their mother needed some time alone.

Elena spent the rest of the day driving aimlessly, trying to find solace in the quiet solitude. Meanwhile, Alex and the children adjusted their plans, opting for a more subdued celebration. They focused on supporting each other, sharing their feelings, and finding comfort in their close-knit family unit.

Though the day didn't go as planned, it became a poignant reminder of the importance of understanding and compassion within a family. Elena's storming out was a cry for help, and Alex's response was a testament to their deep connection and mutual respect.

Chapter 6: Elena's New Beginning

Elena embraced her new job with enthusiasm, finding a renewed sense of purpose and joy in her work. She relished the connections she made with her colleagues, which brought a fresh sense of independence into her life. Free from Alex's constant criticism, Elena rediscovered her self-worth. She began to see herself as a capable and strong individual, no longer overshadowed by negativity. With Alex's oppressive influence diminished, Elena turned her attention to fostering her children's independence and self-confidence. She encouraged Emma and Jake to pursue their interests and make their own decisions, promoting their well-being and growth.

Despite the challenges, Elena's life began to improve. She felt a sense of peace and empowerment that had been missing for so long. She knew that the road ahead would not be easy, but she was determined to create a future where she and her children could thrive without the shadow of Alex's control.

As the therapy sessions continued, Alex requested individual sessions with Dr. Bennett. He claimed he had things he wanted to talk about and work through on his own. Elena was hopeful that this could be a turning point, perhaps a sign that Alex was finally willing to address his deeper issues.

During his first individual session, Dr. Bennett encouraged Alex to open up about what he wanted to discuss.

Dr. Bennett: "Alex, I'm glad you've decided to have these individual sessions. What would you like to focus on?"

Alex sat back, appearing more contemplative than usual.

Alex: "I've been thinking a lot about our sessions. I feel misunderstood, like no one really gets my side of things."

Dr. Bennett: "I understand that feeling. Can you tell me more about why you feel misunderstood?"

Alex took a deep breath, choosing his words carefully.

Alex: "I've always been the one in control. At work, at home... it's just how I'm wired. But lately, I feel like everything is slipping away. Elena's new job, the way she talks to me... it's like I'm losing my place in our relationship."

Dr. Bennett nodded, sensing an opportunity to delve deeper.

Dr. Bennett: "It sounds like control is very important to you. Can you explore why that might be?"

Alex hesitated, then started to speak more candidly.

Alex: "Growing up, my father was very controlling. Nothing I did was ever good enough for him. I swore I'd never be like him, but now I see that I've been controlling in my own way. It's like if I'm not in control, I'm nothing."

Dr. Bennett listened attentively, noting the vulnerability in Alex's voice.

Dr. Bennett: "That sounds like a very painful experience. It's understandable that you might seek control as a way to avoid feeling powerless. But it seems that this need for control is affecting your relationships negatively. How does that realization make you feel?"

Alex looked down, the facade of confidence cracking slightly.

Alex: "It scares me. I don't want to lose Elena, but I don't know how to let go of this need to control everything."

Dr. Bennett saw a glimmer of potential for genuine progress.

Dr. Bennett: "Acknowledging this is a significant first step, Alex. It's important to understand that control doesn't equate to strength or love. Real strength comes from vulnerability and trust. Are you willing to explore ways to build trust and let go of some control?"

Alex nodded slowly.

Alex: "I think I am. But it's hard. I don't even know where to start."

Dr. Bennett: "We can work on this together. It will take time and effort, but it's possible. Let's start by identifying specific situations where you feel the need to control and explore alternative ways to handle them. Can you think of a recent example?"

Alex thought for a moment.

Alex: "When Elena started her new job, I felt like she was slipping away from me. I tried to dismiss her achievements because I felt threatened."

Dr. Bennett: "That's a good example. Instead of dismissing her achievements, what could you do to support her and show that you value her independence?"

Alex sighed, clearly struggling with the idea.

Alex: "I guess I could try to show interest in her work, ask her about her day, and genuinely listen."

Dr. Bennett: "That's a great start. It's about shifting your focus from control to support. By showing genuine interest and listening, you build trust and strengthen your relationship. How do you think Elena would feel if you approached her this way?"

Alex paused, imagining the scenario.

Alex: "She'd probably feel more appreciated and respected. Maybe it would help rebuild some of the trust we've lost."

Dr. Bennett: "Exactly. It's about small, consistent changes. We can work on these strategies and practice them. Over time, you'll find that letting go of control can lead to a more fulfilling relationship for both of you."

As the individual sessions progressed, Alex began to explore his own behavior more deeply. He started to understand the roots of his need for control and how it had impacted his relationship with Elena and their children. Dr. Bennett guided him through exercises in empathy, active listening, and vulnerability.

While Alex struggled with these concepts, he showed a willingness to try. He began to practice being more supportive and less critical, both in therapy and at home. Elena noticed these small changes and felt cautiously optimistic, though she remained guarded.

Elena: "Alex, I've noticed you've been more supportive lately. It means a lot to me."

Alex: "I'm trying, Elena. I know I have a long way to go, but I want us to work."

Through their individual and joint sessions, they both started to see glimmers of hope. It was a difficult journey, but with the help of Dr. Bennett, they were slowly finding a way to rebuild their relationship on a foundation of trust, respect, and mutual support. Elena remained vigilant, knowing that true change would take time and consistency, but she felt stronger and more independent, ready to face whatever came next.

After a few promising sessions where Alex seemed willing to explore his issues, he suddenly dropped the ball and went silent. Despite the progress they had made, his lack of communication left Elena feeling confused and frustrated.

Elena couldn't shake the feeling that Alex's silence was a sign of regression. She worried that he was reverting to old patterns of avoidance and denial rather than confronting the issues that had plagued their relationship. The abruptness of his withdrawal from therapy sessions left her feeling abandoned and uncertain about their future.

"Why did he suddenly stop? Was I expecting too much too soon? Does he even care about making things better?"

Elena reached out to Dr. Bennett, seeking guidance on how to navigate this new challenge. In their next joint session, she expressed her concerns about Alex's withdrawal and the impact it was having on their progress.

Elena: "Dr. Bennett, I don't understand why Alex has gone silent. We were making progress, and now it feels like we're back to square one."

Dr. Bennett: "It's understandable that you're feeling frustrated, Elena. Sometimes, people can feel overwhelmed or resistant to change, especially when facing difficult emotions. Have you tried talking to Alex about how you feel?"

Elena: "I've tried, but he just shuts down. It's like he doesn't want to acknowledge what's happening."

Dr. Bennett: "It sounds like Alex might be struggling with his own internal conflicts. When people face challenges that threaten their sense of control or self-image, they can retreat into silence as a way to avoid confronting those feelings."

Elena: "But where does that leave us? I want to work things out, but I can't do it alone."

Dr. Bennett: "You're absolutely right, Elena. It takes both parties committing to the process for therapy to be effective. It might be helpful to give Alex some space while gently encouraging him to return to therapy when he's ready."

Elena decided to give Alex the space he seemed to need while focusing on her own emotional well-being and that of their children. She continued attending therapy sessions on her own, using the time to explore her own feelings and gain clarity on her priorities moving forward.

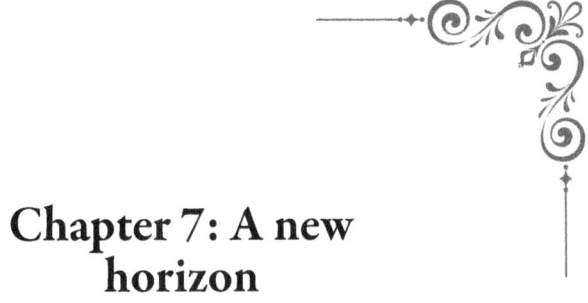

Chapter 7: A new horizon

As time passed, Elena remained open to the possibility of reconciliation, but she also began to consider what a future without Alex might look like. She strengthened her support network, leaned on trusted friends and family, and focused on building her career and personal interests.

While the sudden silence from Alex was a painful setback for Elena, but it also prompted her to prioritize her own needs and emotional health. She realized that she couldn't force Alex to confront his issues or commit to therapy, but she could control how she responded to the situation. Whether Alex eventually returned to therapy or not, Elena was determined to continue her journey of self-discovery and healing, prepared for whatever the future might hold.

After the abrupt silence from Alex and feeling emotionally drained from the uncertainty of their relationship, Elena made a bold decision: she moved to a new city. It was a fresh start, a chance to begin anew without the weight of Alex's controlling behaviour and the disappointments of their past.

Elena's New Beginning:

1. **Exploring Opportunities:** In her new city, Elena threw herself into exploring job opportunities. She updated her resume, networked with professionals in her field, and

attended career fairs and networking events. The change of scenery and the excitement of new possibilities helped lift her spirits.
2. **Finding a Support Network:** Elena actively sought out social activities and groups where she could meet new people and build a support network. Whether it was joining a local book club, taking yoga classes, or volunteering at community events, she embraced opportunities to connect with others who shared her interests.
3. **Embracing Independence:** Living on her own in a new city allowed Elena to rediscover her independence and sense of self. She decorated her new apartment according to her taste, explored local cafes and parks, and enjoyed the freedom to make decisions without second-guessing herself.
4. **Reflecting and Healing:** Away from the familiar surroundings that reminded her of Alex, Elena took time to reflect on her past and focus on her healing journey. She continued attending therapy sessions, now with a new therapist who helped her process the emotions and uncertainties of her recent experiences.
5. **Planning for the Future:** While the future remained uncertain, Elena started to envision possibilities beyond her past relationship with Alex. She set personal and professional goals, such as advancing in her career, pursuing hobbies she had neglected, and fostering a supportive environment for herself and her children.

Challenges and Growth:

Despite the initial challenges of starting over in a new city, Elena found strength in her resilience and determination. Each day brought new opportunities for growth and self-discovery. She faced moments of doubt and loneliness but drew on her inner strength and the support of her newfound community to keep moving forward.

Hope for the Future:

Elena didn't know what the future held, but she felt a sense of optimism and hope for the first time in a long while. The decision to move had been daunting, but it was also liberating. She was no longer defined by her past with Alex; instead, she was creating a future filled with possibilities, independence, and the promise of a life where she could thrive on her own terms.

Chapter 8: The Awakening

In the quiet moments of solitude that followed her decision to move to a new city, Elena found herself embarking on a profound journey of healing and spiritual awakening. Days stretched into weeks, and with each passing moment, she began to reclaim fragments of herself that had been obscured by the shadows of a tumultuous relationship. The echoes of emotional manipulation and conditional love, wielded by Alex, slowly dissolved as she immersed herself in therapy, reconnected with supportive friends and family, and rediscovered the passions that once ignited her soul.

Elena's story is not merely one of resilience but a testament to the transformative power of spiritual awakening. Eckhart Tolle's seminal work, *The Power of Now*, resonated deeply with her during this pivotal time. In Tolle's teachings, Elena found solace and guidance as she navigated the labyrinth of her emotions and thoughts. The concept of presence, central to Tolle's philosophy, became her anchor—an invaluable tool in unraveling the complexities of her past and embracing the beauty of the present moment.

Elena learned to discern the subtle manipulations woven into the fabric of her relationship with Alex. His expressions of love, once perceived as genuine, revealed themselves as instruments of control—conditions imposed upon her to maintain his dominance. Through the lens of Tolle's teachings, she understood that true love transcends conditions; it flows freely, nurturing growth and mutual respect. This realization empowered Elena to break free from the chains of emotional dependency, forging a path towards authentic self-expression and self-love.

As she delved deeper into her spiritual journey, Elena cultivated mindfulness and presence as guiding principles. Meditation became a daily ritual, a sacred space where she could quiet the noise of her mind and listen to the whispers of her heart. In these moments of stillness, she uncovered insights and revelations that illuminated her path forward. She learned to honor her intuition, trusting its wisdom to navigate life's uncertainties with grace and clarity.

Elena's journey of healing and spiritual growth was not without its challenges. There were moments of doubt and fear, echoes of the past threatening to pull her back into familiar patterns. Yet, armed with the teachings of Eckhart Tolle and supported by a newfound community of kindred spirits, she persevered. She embraced vulnerability as a catalyst for growth, dismantling the walls she had built around her heart and allowing herself to experience life fully, without reservation.

Her journey was not just about overcoming past wounds but about embracing the profound potential within herself. It was a journey towards wholeness, where every step forward was a testament to her strength and resilience. Through introspection and self-discovery, Elena redefined her sense of purpose and embraced a future filled with boundless possibilities.

Elena's story is a poignant reminder of the transformative power of spiritual awakening. Guided by Eckhart Tolle's teachings, she navigated the complexities of healing and growth with courage and grace. Her journey serves as an inspiration to all who seek to reclaim their authentic selves and live with presence, authenticity, and love.

Epilogue

Years later, Elena found herself at another art gallery, this time as an artist in her own right. Her paintings, rich with emotion and depth, were a testament to her journey. She had learned to love herself, flaws and all, and to recognize the difference between genuine love and the toxic allure of a narcissistic relationship.

As she mingled with the guests, Elena felt a sense of peace and fulfillment. She had not only survived but thrived, turning her pain into beauty and her struggle into strength. And as she gazed at her reflection in the glass, she saw a woman who had finally found herself.

About the Author

Rachel Mann is an author and passionate advocate for personal growth and resilience. With a background in consulting and a deep interest in psychology, she writes about the complexities of relationships, the power of self-discovery, and the strength that comes from breaking free. Rachel's work explores the intersection of emotional healing and personal empowerment, and her debut novel, *Twisted Pearl of the Prairies*, delves into the journey of reclaiming one's identity in the face of manipulation. When she's not writing, Rachel enjoys traveling, painting, journaling, and exploring new ways to foster well-being and connection.

Read more at www.rachelhor.com.

www.ingramcontent.com/pod-product-compliance
Ingram Content Group UK Ltd.
Pitfield, Milton Keynes, MK11 3LW, UK
UKHW042216291224
452836UK00004B/158